CW01080301

Tales of our Times

For my most excellent
friend

Kate

from Margaret 22/6/04.
xx

LET'S FIND OUT WHAT EVERYONE IS DOING

AND THEN . . .

STOP EVERYONE FROM DOING IT

(*Let's Stop Somebody* A P Herbert)

Tales of our Times

A Collection of Old and New Fairy Stories

By
Margaret Whyte, Linda Thatcher and Katie-Ellen Hazeldine

With a contribution by
Quentin Hughes

And dedicated to the memory of his mother
Lindsay Waller
22nd October 1945 – 15th March 1997

The Pentland Press
Edinburgh – Cambridge – Durham – USA

First published in 1998 by
The Pentland Press Ltd
1 Hutton Close,
South Church
Bishop Auckland
Durham

ISBN 1-85821-570-6

Typeset in Monotype Fournier

by Carnegie Publishing, 18 Maynard St, Preston
Printed and bound by Antony Rowe Ltd, Chippenham

Contents

Illustrations

Foreword

ome years ago, my friend gave me a copy of a version of "The Three Little Pigs" which her son, then aged 14, had written as a school exercise. I was struck by the implications of rewriting these tales of the universal condition of Humankind, so as to reaffirm their relevance to experience today, and to lend greater credibility to the characters involved.

Some years later, my friend Lindsay asked if I still had a copy of her son's story. We were discussing it as an example of a literary medium which could bear further development. Lindsay and I agreed to try our hand at some well known fairy stories, giving them a modern twist. Unfortunately, Lindsay was very ill with the brain tumour which led to her death shortly afterwards, and beyond writing herself. It is impossible to convey in a few words the amazing character of Lindsay. She was above all eager. Eager for experience for herself and others but above all eager to see people, especially young people, develop talents they would never have suspected they had. She was an indefatigable and relentless pursuer of opportunities for others. I went ahead with a couple of stories and showed them to Linda, my close friend and colleague. She immediately responded with "Snowbright and the Seven Giants" and "Jack and the Beans". By now the ball was rolling. My daughter Katie-Ellen was inspired to have a go, and also volunteered to illustrate the stories, with a combination of childish technique and adult insight, to complement our treatment of the medium.

Lindsay died. As a testament to her way of getting others to have a go, this book is dedicated to her memory.

As for the stories themselves, we have attempted to use the originals in such a way as to illustrate how they successfully cross time and geographical boundaries, as also literary boundaries of fantasy and "faction". If the fairy stories are universally valid, we reckoned that if we remained faithful to their import, our versions would not detract from their original magic. They are very dense, in line with the tradition of the short story, and any opacity should be resolved on subsequent readings. Each has several messages as well as a main theme. All are based on personal experience, and we hope that the reader will approve of the issues highlighted as worthy of reflection for the times in which we live.

Margaret Whyte
August 1997

I

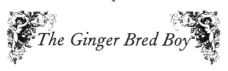

The Ginger Bred Boy

"What though the field be lost?
All is not lost – the unconquerable will
And study of revenge, immortal hate
And courage never to submit or yield:
And what else not to be overcome?"

Milton, *Paradise Lost*, Book 1

Once upon a time in California, a very successful architect team of husband and wife decided that after all they would like a little boy, and these days there was no such thing as leaving things too late. They wanted him to be fair and blue eyed and very intelligent. They wanted him to be an Arian and to be athletic. So they consulted a Grand Wizard who was famous for managing these things and he promised to deliver the goods, as designed, for a price. They did all he told them and went through all the processes and on the first day of April a little boy duly arrived.

He was a day early but who could carp about so little after so much? From the moment of his arrival, it was clear that he was fair and gave promise of considerable strength of mind and body. Immediately after his birth, he looked straight at his parents, yelled loudly, sucked greedily, filled his nappy often and with gusto, yelled, fed again, was heartily sick, and so on. He grew very rapidly, was awake and active for most of the twenty-four hours in the day and developed early and fast. By three months he was crawling. By four months he was manipulating electric sockets and at six months he walked. At one year he was avidly studying the adverts on the TV and it dawned on his still proud parents that he engaged on househunts to try and locate what he had seen on the Box. He refused to waste time by such stupidities as sitting on knees and made sure of not repeating stories by tearing out the page as soon as he knew its content. At eighteen months his parents took to consulting other Grand Wizards, for a price, about how to arrive at a modus vivendi with their son. Friends and relatives had stopped accepting invitations to their home and they had gotten through seventeen nannies and reached stalemate with their last

advert. The agencies had taken them off their books. The wife was forced to stay at home one morning after drawing a complete blank with all attempts to summon aid. After that day, surveying the contents of the fridge, mostly in the trash can, which overflowed all over the kitchen floor, the Meissen dinner service arranged on the dining room furniture, reached where necessary with the aid of chairs, and laid out with antique toy soldiers marshalled on the plates, the toilet blocked with her makeup (about 300 dollars worth), all bed-clothes pulled off to make bouncy castles and the contents of the cupboard-under-the-sink bottles used to clean the sitting room carpet, for the child moved much faster than she did, she phoned her husband in hysterics to come home RIGHT AWAY.

Next day she went to work, leaving him to experience the companionship of this intelligent and athletic child. At 11am she received a phone call from her husband to say that right now the child was copying the pictures on the wall using excrement and a wooden spoon underneath the originals. Was this normal behaviour? A Grand Wizard, immediately contacted, for a price, said it was indeed normal. Because their son was so physically advanced he could carry out what less able and therefore more repressed children could only dream of.

After a Grand Discussion on the return of the wife from work that day, when each had apportioned relative responsibility for the exact designation of the child, it was decided that both should take leave from work until some more suitable arrangement could be sorted out. Long years till the minimum age for boarding school could not be faced. Both simultaneously hit on the brilliant idea of getting in a foreign nanny from a disadvantaged part of the world. They were aware of the implications in the kind of arrangements made by some of these agencies, for a price. Such may imply that the nanny could not leave her post for fear of the booking agency which would receive part of her wages as fees for finding the job, advancing the loan for the journey, for a suitable wardrobe, providing forged proof of qualifications, and any other facilitations.

What a brilliant idea! Maria from Manila duly arrived, all humble smiles, and expressions of delight with the prodigious child she was privileged to tend. The fact that she spoke hardly any English mattered not at all. After a week, Maria was heard weeping in her room. It was very loud weeping indeed to be heard over the vigorous singing of the infant who of course did not go to bed and who was at that precise point in time engaged in lubricating the door handle receiver in the door jamb with a couple of slugs he had brought earlier from the patio, for that purpose.

The parents feared Maria would attempt a break-out despite their calculations. As they listened to the commotion upstairs they simultaneously had another brilliant idea. What if they allowed Maria to go home, taking the boy, and they would send her her wages OVER THERE?! They could set up a generous capital amount, for immediate use, a good allowance to be paid directly to Maria, and what financial arrangements would make it responsible and advantageous, so to speak. As always, they understood that everything has its price.

Without further ado, up they went and conveyed to her the offer to restore her to the bosom of her family and mother country where she could continue to earn her living without this exile. The only stipulated condition was that she must absolutely accept full custody of her charge, for a price. Maria, who had no doubt of the ability of her father and brothers to deal appropriately with this ginger monster-demon with the pale blue eyes and no lashes or brows, readily agreed to accept a single ticket for herself and the infant to Manila, and the parents' promise to set up a large capital sum for immediate access and a further trust fund, contracts for which would accompany her on the plane. All happened as they promised except that professional commitments prevented the parents from visiting their son, which may only have succeeded in disturbing and destabilising him in his new home anyway.

Their business prospered. They designed and built a new house which won fame and awards, some two hours drive from the last. They omitted to forward to Manila their new address. The correspondence, infrequent from the first and unsatisfactory because of Maria's illiteracy, had long ceased. Only the capital accounts and trust funds showed the contacts through regular withdrawals.

They had omitted as well the precaution of changing their son's nationality and, some twenty years or so later, they received a phone call from the American Consulate in Manila. The caller was instructed to say that their son was temporarily leaving Manila for business reasons and would arrive in two days time. The official on the phone was a bit cagey with additional information, saying merely that he had been asked to ensure that they should expect a visit from their son. When asked to enquire after Maria and her family, the Consulate replied that enquiries to the Filipino police could elicit no information on that subject.

The next day more than twenty phone calls from complete strangers from as far afield as Bolivia, Mexico, several cities of North America, and Rome were received by the company secretary of the parents' firm, asking whether Mr Fox had arrived yet. No numbers were left.

Frantic calls to the Consulate in Manila brought no enlightenment except that their son, known to all over there as Mr Fox, was a prominent businessman with a network of very influential friends. They also intimated that he was travelling abroad to follow up some contacts and leaving Manila on the personal advice of the President himself. He was also known to be very rich.

With some trepidation the parents prepared necessary stories with which to receive their long absent son. They need not have worried. He himself called from the airport from which he was taking a hire car. Had the Consul called? He was sorry to cause them any inconvenience. He hoped they would forgive him for not writing nor contacting them before especially after such generous provision as they had made. He hoped they would think he had put it all to good use. And now, continued his smooth, light and pleasant voice, with no trace of any other than a well-bred Southern States accent, he could not wait to see them again and thank them properly for all their careful arrangements for his upbringing.

As he descended from the taxi as it crunched to a halt on their red chip drive in the early evening, they could see that he was all they had designed. Tall, with a mane of red-gold hair, powerfully built, dressed in creme shantung, and carrying a large blue holdall and a crocodile bag, he cast keen eyes over their white and glass house as he paid the driver and straightened with his luggage. Enough for a weekend. How tactful not to bring more. How right to have given their son more space and status to grow up in his own way where he could be himself rather than to have made him miserable trying to fit into a society that was all too sure of what people should become. How fortunate it is to hit on the right solution without always understanding exactly why.

Mr Fox needed only a weekend to sort out his parents and encourage them to broaden their horizons as he had done. He sent them on a round of visits all over the world where they made contact with all his friends who had need of architects to take care of the unusual requirements of their accommodation, which needed high security, luxurious living accommodation and the latest communication systems. They travelled by private planes arranged by their son and his contacts. Having appointed their son as Managing Director in their absence and in the event of any unfortunate mishap, you may be surprised to know that it was a full six months before their private jet was lost somewhere over the Andes. Their company, with an enlarged team of architects from all over the world, went on to diversify into construction, mining and various other enterprises, some more obviously connected than others.

They had surely bred a winner, who, like his parents, understood very well that everything has its price.

_____

Margaret Whyte

II

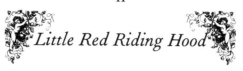

Little Red Riding Hood

here once was a girl who lived in a forest with her mother and father. Her father worked as a logger and they lived in a tied house where their only neighbour was her grandmother who was the widow of a forestry worker. Grandmother still lived in the house which was no longer required for a worker in the dwindling forest. The girl was not at all lonely for she had a vivid imagination and the forest where she grew up held no fears for her. It was people she was not so keen on. They thought her queer with her collections of beetles and amphibia and her declared preference for eating fungi, which she sold locally for pocket money.

Every week her mother sent her to visit her grandmother with supplies of home baking and staples from the nearest village store. The girl detested these visits for her grandmother's way of eating disgusted her. She always grumbled, spoke in detail about aches and pains, produced bits of broken photographs of her dead husband and a little boy who had drowned in the flooded beck.

There was only one nice thing in her grandmother's house that the girl asked to see every time and that was a gold and coral and turquoise necklace that the long dead grandfather had brought back from some foreign war. The grandmother indicated, but never actually promised, that one day this would come to her. Neither did she ever offer to let her try it on. It was out of keeping with the assorted decay in the rest of the house and the only bright thing.

Every time she set off to the grandmother's house, her mother warned her to go straight there, not to step off the path and not to stop for any stranger. She was never to be rude, but neither was she ever to give more information than necessary to anyone for "one never knew", whatever that may mean. Actually, the girl understood her mother's meaning very well. For years now she had known the local wolf. He was the last of his kind in all the forests around. He was both timid and curious and used to follow her to see what she was doing when she went the round of her traps and poked about in the boggy bits behind the banks of the beck. One day she cornered him and asked whether he had nothing better to do than spy on her. The wolf confessed to boredom, loneliness and not infrequent hunger. After that she sometimes slipped him some of the baking and an occasional apple and onion from her grandmother's supplies. He especially appreciated a bag of beefy crisps and in return the girl asked him to show her where she could find the best blewitts and chanterelles. Having given him these to smell once, he caught on straight away.

The wolf took to hanging round the house hoping she was coming out, but on the odd occasion he was seen by the girl's parents, they said nothing, so as not to frighten her. If she caught him near the house, he got a good slap. She was afraid her parents would not let her leave the house if they thought their daughter was going out with a wolf.

There came a time when the girl fancied another sort of wolf and took to hanging around the village with a group of other girls, taunting the local boys. One, more curious and daring than the rest, decided to chance his luck with the queer girl from the forest who was pretty enough to offset derision from his

Wolf liked crisps ...

mates, and always had a bob or two from her sales of forest fare. Anyway, he was a bit of a loner too.

When she dated him in the forest, the wolf made three and a crowd. The wolf decided after a couple of rebuffs to see if the grandmother would accept a visit from him and maybe give him a cake or even a bag of crisps. He sat outside the grandmother's door until she came out and thought he was a dog. He politely withstood a couple of shooings but was not put out when he crept in. The grandmother was very short-sighted and did not believe in wolves. Eventually, after a couple of visits, he thought he was quids in. He was allowed to lie on the hearthrug. He was given the remains of her meals, which glory be included bones, and thought her place was marvellous. He wondered why he had not thought of trying the grandmother years ago instead of wasting his time with her mean and demanding granddaughter. He resolved to bring her the funny smelling things in future as a reward for the new warm home he intended to be accepted into.

The new partnership went very well. The grandmother was very pleased with his offerings but was unable to recognise the deathcaps he brought her by mistake, carefully wrapped in a fallen leaf as the girl had taught him. It was the girl's father who found her all twisted and stiff in death. The wolf in horror had done a swift bunk and did not stop moving until several forests later. The girl claimed the necklace which she wore shortly after when she had to get married thanks to the courtship in the forest. Red Riding Hood never missed the wolf. He died not long after, pining for the rug and bones that had eluded him.

Margaret Whyte

III

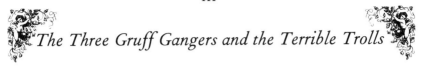

The Three Gruff Gangers and the Terrible Trolls

"Each man kills the thing he loves".

Oscar Wilde, *The Ballad of Reading Gaol*

---

here are three Gruff Gangers dressed all in green armour whose mission is to keep the land open to the People. Over thick red socks, they wear huge boots, with which they cover ground in great leaps and bounds. Especially they are fond of high places, forests and woodland, river banks, bogs and marshes and all places where the wild things are. Wherever they go they are dogged by three Terrible Trolls called Enseesee, Elay, and Seepeearee.

There is a famous meadow which the three Terrible Trolls are irrevocably determined to keep free from the Gruff Gangers and all of their kind. It is especially beautiful, rich in flowers, and many kinds of rare and delicate animals. It has its own name: Essessie. It is guarded by a bridge which crosses a deep and weedy stream. Its other boundary is a steep cliff, densely wooded, in a great amphitheatre, sweeping in a great arc. The Terrible Trolls rush to guard the bridge whenever the Three Gruff Gangers are in its vicinity. They sit under the bridge ready to rush out to do battle. They have spray paint and huge pairs of scissors to combat the awesome maps wielded by the Gruff Gangers in their gauntleted hands. The bridge is barred with quarter staff and gate covered in barbed wire.

Down come the Gruff Gangers onto the bridge. Bang goes the boot of the first as he steps onto the plank. Out pops the first Troll.

"Ghastly Gangers bog off now.
This special meadow's our domain.
Your hated boots do not allow
The snake and slowworm to remain".

He brandishes his spray paint with a flourish, but the first Ganger snarls

"We mean to pass, you ugly trolls.

~ 9 ~

Elay.....
One lonely
troll
on patrol

The land is not yours to protect.
The people's rights define our goals
And all free land we will connect".

The first Troll sprays the Ganger luminous pink and thrusts at him with his huge scissors. The bridge is clear. The Gangers retreat, for they cannot be seen in luminous pink. But they will try again after their comrade has been tended and cleaned up. They come the next day and the second Gruff Ganger puts her foot on the bridge.

"Get out of my way you fascist trolls.
We're coming whether you like it or not.
Your day is done. Consult the polls.
You're nothing but a piece of snot."

The Trolls have prepared for this onslaught and produce three huge pink balloons wound round each other in an offensive way. No holds can be barred in so deadly a duel for the land. The Ganger turns her back on the bridge in disgust and retreats with her companions to make a Formal Complaint. The next day, battle is joined once more. The third and Gruffest Ganger, whose boot has banged on the head of many a mountain and revealed the feet of clay in many a river path, now moves onto the bridge.

"Bastard Trolls get off our patch.
In us you'll find you've met your match.
Plants and worms make sound green sense,
But human rights take precedence.

A contract's out for your demise.
The footpath's here despite your lies.
The record lodges with the Law.
Now scram before we shed the gore."

And with this the Gruff Gangers all pound onto the planks of the bridge which collapses. They are drowned and two of the Trolls are crushed beneath the mess of wood and Gangers. A big stone monument stands on the spot where the Martyrs of the Freeways died and the death of the Terrible Trolls is celebrated, for is not the meadow for all? Long after it has disappeared in a muddy mess, the memory of its winning will live in hearts and minds as a great triumph for the Gangers on behalf of the people.

That still leaves one solitary Troll to guard the wonderful places where the

Gruff Gangers have not yet claimed their right to go. Elay is very lonely and he feels his job is far too much for one Troll.

Margaret Whyte

The Three Ramblers Geoff

"*All Nature wears one universal grin*".

Henry Fielding , *Tom Thumb the Great*

hree bearded ramblers were trotting across the meadow one fine afternoon. They loved to explore and they deplored the fencing off, by farmers or bureaucrats, of so many pretty places which were their national heritage. Last year, they had encountered a farmer who had proved to be culturally challenged. He had responded to their pertinent observations that they could not be trespassing if the land was morally theirs, by attacking them with a muckspreader. Big Geoff, who had the widest beard in a wicked shade of ginger, much envied by the other two, had written to his MP to place the atrocity on record.

The MP wrote back to express his regret that he could not condone trespass on privately owned land, much as he deplored the farmer's action.

Big Geoff, Medium Geoff and Little Geoff had heard of the wondrous June blooming of monkey orchids in the Turvey Tussock boglands, and they made their plans. Video cameras, badminton racquets for walking on bog, Kendal mintcake and isotonic drinks were all packed. Recycled toilet paper in a pleasant shade known as "natural oatmeal" was a considerate precaution. (No lurid pink must be allowed to frighten the wildlife.) The final item was a can of green spraypaint.

The first attempt to bar them from paradise took the form of a sign saying, "Please do not enter this designated conservation area. Rare flowers in bloom." Big Geoff sprayed over this with the words " Flowers for free. Free the flowers."

Half a mile later, they encountered a countryside warden, who attempted to remonstrate with them. The conversation became heated. He was alone and minus a muckspreader and their patience was running low. So they debagged him and sprayed his bottom green. They took his trousers and underpants with them to inhibit his options for follow-up action.

The final obstacle was another sign which read, "Dangerous bog. Do not enter."

No question of needing the badminton raquets. The Geoffs understood the game.

"Ha Ha," said Little Geoff. "Whatever will they think of next?"

"Gloop Gloop," said the bog.

K-E Hazeldine

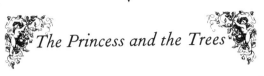

The Princess and the Trees

"Woodman spare that tree".

George Pope Morris

t was in the news every day. Protracted resistance to the construction of a bypass to the east of the village of Baglady-on-Straw. The bypass would cut a searing swathe through ancient woodland, all to accommodate even more moronic nineteen-year-old male drivers with gelled heads. Resistance from many villagers was hugely strengthened by the environmental guerrillas, Bigroot and Soilsoldier, handsome modern heroes, and their band of followers. These had created a woodland citadel from which to defy the

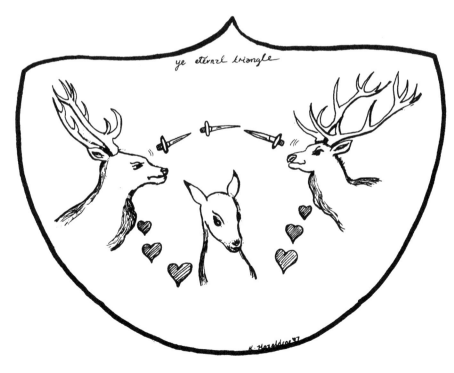

"yellow hats" and "clipboards", and their perplexed stooges, the police. Shop-keepers, teachers, students, readers of *Watership Down* and *Silent Spring*, even solicitors and quarry managers could be counted amongst their growing numbers, although these may have been spies.

It took dedication to sleep rough and be smelly, though wetwipes were a help. It took stamina to tolerate conditions not knowing how long the situation would continue. Some people who joined the protest were not really prepared for this. One such person was young Sapphira Nisbit, daughter of a wealthy city banker. She had decided to disappear from home during the university summer vacation in order to join the protest. (What would have been the use of all her riding lessons if there were no longer woods to trek through?) She was delighted to have the opportunity of upsetting her conformist family for a worthy cause, but yearned for home comforts after a day. Hot baths, cool sheets and hot buttered toast, cool Fanta with a green stripy straw.

Now Sapphira was a knockout as far as men were concerned. Bigroot took an instant fancy to her, to the despair of his other devoted female followers. He renamed her Dryad, and it was transparently clear, whenever he turned his eyes upon her that his thoughts ran along the themes of sowing, propagation and so forth. However, Bigroot, for the present, concentrated his prodigious energies and tactical genius upon the main objective.

Upwind of this increasingly mighty gathering was an hotel. The hotel proprietor, Mr Chance, had great hopes that the bypass would bring him more business, conveniently situated as the hotel would be for its traffic. He and his wife had recently made many improvements in the hope of being upgraded by the RAC and local Tourist Board. They could now offer percale pillow cases embroidered with the words "Goodnight" on one side and " Sweet Dreams" on the other, breakfast eggs which were free-range, Costa Rican coffee, and sparkling new bidets for all with gold-plated taps.

Their son was twenty and something of a lad. They did wish he would take an interest in nicer girls than the vulgar Madonna look-alikes he favoured. These lowered the tone in the hotel bar. Lately one of these girls had succumbed to intoxication and had performed a knickerless cancan which the other guests disastrously mistook for organised entertainment. The episode cost them their Highly Commended rating, and to their chagrin the hotel was demoted to Commended (*review pending), – hence the new bidets.

After this, they had extracted a promise from their son that from now on his girlfriends would arrive knickered and stay sober and knickered while on the premises. Any deviation from this and Sonny-boy would be permanently denied access to the Supuki Fourtrak, stressed his exasperated father.

One rainy miserable evening, a cool, gorgeous, and extremely well-spoken young lady arrived in reception, wanting a room for the night. She was lucky to be accommodated without a booking, but the flow of bookings was not as good as it had been before the *incident*. Sonny-boy was agog but she obviously thought he was some lower life-form, such as a porter. She negligently handed him a surprisingly scruffy rucksack to take upstairs. She requested *pâté de foie gras*, toast and Assam tea, to be delivered to her room toute de suite, and she tipped him liberally, to his embarrassment.

Could she be an undercover hotel inspector, Mr and Mrs Chance asked one another? Her attitude did not tally with her luggage. Could this be the longed-for opportunity to get back their " Highly Recommended"? The guest was certainly demanding. She buzzed for aromatherapy bath oils (citrus, please, I need revivifying). She buzzed for cocoa and shortbread, and the latest issue of *Marie Claire* (not available? Why not?).

Sapphira fully intended to eat a very early breakfast and to rejoin her fellow protesters in the hope that they would not have missed her. She simply could not manage it. One night sleeping rough was enough, but she had persevered and endured four nights of it. Surely she was doing her bit? One more evening would set her up for the rest of the protest.

Bigroot and Soilsoldier were planning a diversionary tactic that would detract the police away from the roadsite so that they could trash as much enemy equipment as possible. (Besides, trees were not the only claim upon their consciences). Adjacent to the nearby hotel was a wicked venison farm, The protesters could make two protests simultaneously. Soilsoldier picked up his mobile phone, gulped the last of his acorn coffee and dialled the number for the local newspaper.

Next evening, Sapphira, clad in some amazing crumple-free dress, sat alone at her table in the hotel restaurant. She scanned the menu. Sonny-boy hovered in attendance, hopelessly stricken, and acting as personal factotum at the instigation of his parents, though he needed no persuasion.

It was a Saturday, and the hotel would be busy. The Chances felt very hopeful that their menu and service would do them credit. Sapphira, with a pang of conscience at her treachery, but unable to resist, ordered lobster bisque, to be followed by roast venison with creamed potatoes and artichokes.

As she sipped her lobster bisque her mind began to clamour. Her parents, the protest, what was she doing here, was she unprincipled, programmed for reactionary decadence? The clamour in her mind grew until it blotted out all other sound. The French windows shattered inwards. My goodness, she realised. The noise was not in her head at all!

Seconds later a herd of forty-seven irate deer stampeded through the restaurant, scattering croutons, tables and diners like chaff. After them came a psychedelically decorated van, beeping its horn, driven by Bigroot, with a dozen reporters and an excited press photographer beside him. Right up to the dessert trolley they drove. The uproar was incredible. Frantic deer escaped into the lobby and bar, to the terror of all bipeds. The occupants of the van spilled out and declaimed the rights of deer, using a loudhailer while flashbulbs illuminated the scene for posterity. The most sensational picture was taken when Bigroot and Sonny-boy encountered one another and instantly engaged in mutually antagonistic physical interaction while deer leaped hither and thither in the background.

The police were swiftly on their way, in such numbers that the protesters' task force, led by Soilsoldier, had quite a reasonable opportunity to wreak havoc upon some earthmoving equipment. Meanwhile, in the hotel, deer grazed quietly on peanutted carpets.

Sapphira was greatly impressed and excited by the daring of Bigroot, and he, whilst deploring her incorrigible decadence, was not, on a hormonal level, averse to her dress and chignon. They escaped the scene in the Supuki Four-trak.

It was a typical instance of the Law of Sod, that a hotel inspector was indeed resident at the hotel that very night. He had been looking forward to his roast venison, but all he received was a hoof-print on his derriere, and that does not form part of any criterion for a Highly Commended grade, even when arnica is readily supplied.

K-E Hazeldine

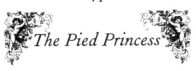

VI

The Pied Princess

"An event has happened upon which it is difficult to speak and impossible to be silent."

Edmund Burke, 1789

---

nce in The Land Of Hope And Glory there ruled a troubled queen. Although the people believed that she and her family ruled in name only because the country was a constitutional monarchy, the power and influence of the family was enormous. This power was exercised for the good of the country as well as for fun and it took mountains of cash to oil its wheels. The cash came from Queenie tithes levied on the people on sales of scratch cards and jelly products, though the income from jelly had fallen dramatically in recent years for unknown reasons. The Queen was worried that this year she would not be able to afford her customary ton of truffles, so vital for securing the goodwill of foreign potentates at palace banquets. There was no help for it but to raise the Queenie tithes. This was bound to prove unpopular in a country weakened by recent civil war between the Pinks and the Turquoises (resolved by forming a government that was Sky-Blue Pink with Yellow dots). She therefore decided on a publicity campaign that would stir up her popularity first.

The instrument of the campaign was to be her daughter, the Pied Princess. She was a striking figure. She was six feet tall and weighed a little over six stone. She had a peculiarity of always wearing exquisitely cut parti-coloured clothes in red and yellow with a lion rampant on each lapel. This was, in essence, the national flag, which she had adapted. She was a major sponsor of the fashion industry which, being a huge national earner, made her the best choice. The Queen's other daughter, the Princess of Tarts, was more fun but not so popular, owing to her love of practical jokes, such as importing ten thousand crates of pigeons into the Capital (to keep council employees in work, she said).

The Pied Princess was given her instructions. "I am afraid you must simply get out there and do some hob-nobbing with frightful commoners. It may stick

in your craw my dear, but he who pays the piper, alas, gets to call the tune. Make sure not to forget your pomander."

It was decided that the Princess would call first at Hamlyn-on-Sea because it was the busiest trading port and contact point with the Continent. The Princess went walkabout and visited a number of collections of distressed people of different varieties before calling in at a trade exhibition down at the quayside.

Here catastrophe struck in the form of a tiny, silent bite of a flea. The flea had recently left home. Home had been a black ship's rat (rattus rattus) on a recently arrived B&Ono Ferry from the Continent. The rat was no longer home because it had died of Teutonic plague and lay even now in a box of apples bound for a major supermarket chain.

The flea found the Princess very comfortable and decided to stay put. This resulted in several unflattering paparazzi snaps as she tried discreetly to locate the source of the itching that tormented her armpit, her thigh and so forth.

When she arrived home two days later, the Pied princess was feeling under the weather (which was uncomfortably hot and sticky). Pausing only to pat the Queen's favourite whippets, Brussels and Luxembourg, she went to bed with a hot lemon drink.

Horrible tragedy swiftly uncoiled itself. Luxembourg happened to nip Mr Lee Thum Suk, a visiting dignitary from Diorea. The flea was practically on its last gasp by now but it still had enough zest for life to add its own nip and to find Mr Lee Thum Suk reasonably tasty though a wee bit tougher than the Princess.

Oh dear. The rest is too grim to chronicle. Suffice it to say that Bestminster Abbey was stuffed full before the ghastly plague was wrestled to extinction by the Fire Brigade, this proving more effective than all the doctors and antibiotics in the Land of Hope and Glory.

The dynasty was no more. The unthinkable had happened.

Marchioness Twatcher, experienced stateswoman, seized the moment. She dashed out from cover, like a moray eel from a hole, for a coup which turned the Sky-Blue Pink with Yellow dots Party to Indigo. And she snaffled the Queen's collection of Hermes scarves, which she had coveted during long years of second position power. And, wise precaution, she outlawed flea circuses, and she banned Europe too.

_____

K-E Hazeldine

Cybele suffers a crushing defeat

VII

Rapunzel

"They have sown the wind and they shall reap the whirlwind"

Hosea 8, vii

---

nce in Central Europe an aid worker adopted a baby and later brought her home to England. The aid worker, Cybele, was deeply interested in all things "close to nature" except for men. Much as she valued certain individuals as fellow campaigners in a cruel world, she preferred a crisp green salad in olive oil and balsamic vinegar dressing.

She was a partner in a small organic vegetable nursery and she called the baby "Rapunzel" after her favourite radishes. When Rapunzel went to school it was not long before she was nicknamed Radish by horrid little Clint McCluskey. When she was seventeen he called her Ravish because she was svelte with long blonde hair. However, his new-found civility profited him not at all. In the eyes of Rapunzel he remained a dung beetle.

Cybele would not let Rapunzel have her hair cut, though Rapunzel longed for a trendier style. She would not let her stay out after eight, or drink alcopops, or have a boyfriend, however platonic. Cybele was determined that no harm would befall her darling through any negligence on her part.

This state of affairs continued until Rapunzel was twenty-five when she decided to assert herself by accepting a dinner invitation from a good-looking hairdresser. Cybele accepted the news quietly, to Rapunzel's surprise and relief. When she was twenty she had made a similar bid for freedom and Cybele had shut her in the greenhouse all day. She had had nothing but raw marrow to eat.

The young man now presenting himself owned a smart salon. He had won prizes for hairdressing. However, he was not an effete young man. He was athletic and keen on rockclimbing. He had noticed Rapunzel looking wistfully into his shop window (Cybele restricted her pocket money) and, admiring her cheekbones, invited her in to act as a model. With delight, Rapunzel agreed to a pixie-cut, but as soon as it was done, she began to hyperventilate on his linoleum in terror at Cybele's anticipated reaction. The temporary solution was enormous hair extensions which could be removed when she found the courage to tell Cybele.

Rapunzel sang like a bird to the karaoke machine in her bedroom as she prepared for the evening *date*. Cybele had gone round to a friend's house for a relaxing tarot session, so she had said.

Imagine the mortification of Rapunzel when the doorbell rang and she found herself locked in, and the keys nowhere to be found! The downstairs windows were locked too.

"Fret not, my ravishing one!" sang out Damien, excited by this challenge. "What about the upstairs windows?"

Shortly afterwards, a young man could be spotted creeping up the wall like a fly on a piece of upright jammy toast. Rapunzel had wound the hair extensions around the hooks that held the curtain tie-backs and Damien hauled himself up on these with confident foolhardiness.

Cybele meanwhile was sipping chamomile tea and poring over her tarot cards. Turning over the last card, she was thunderstruck to read that the cards predicted success for a rival in an affair of the heart. Bidding her friend a hasty farewell, she rattled off for home in her antediluvian Citroen.

She arrived at the door just as the hair extensions gave way and Damien flailed his way wildly downwards and landed upon her. He sustained a bruised coccyx and whiplash injuries to the neck. Cybele did not fare so well. With a thin batsqueak, she entered upon another plane of consciousness, from which dimension she was powerless to prevent subsequent romantic developments.

The tarot cards had not warned her that her defeat would be such a crushing one.

K-E Hazeldine

VIII

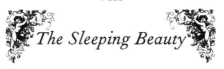 The Sleeping Beauty

"Establishment of Truth depends on destruction of Falsehood continually,

On circumcision, not on Virginity, O Reasoners of Albion".

William Blake, *Jerusalem*, Chapter 3, lines 65–66

I t was the showbiz wedding of the year. Anyone who was anyone was there. Arnie King was marrying Regina Roberts. He was drop dead gorgeous, tall, dark, with a body weight trained to perfection, adored by the millions of fans who flooded to his action movies. She had a face and body to die for, but was nevertheless a serious actress. She only did "meaningful" films, and although they inevitably involved "getting her kit off", this was never, never done gratuitously but always in the interest of Art.

The wedding was just perfect. The sky was blue, the breeze was balmy, the food delicious, and the champagne chilled to exactly the right temperature. The guests were rich, famous, interesting, witty, well connected or eccentric. Indeed, some of them were all of these things. Arnie and Regina were so

overwhelmed by the perfection of themselves and it all, that when they tumbled into bed in the small hours of the morning, they quite forgot about precautions. And so it was that, nine months later, their perfectly beautiful baby daughter was born.

They decided to call her Princess Beauty. This may seem a strange name to you, but this story is set in America, where Earl and Duke are common first names, and wasn't there a rock star called Prince? As for the name Beauty, that came from her father's pet name for her.

The baby's christening a year later saw another great gathering of the Hollywood glitterati who came once again to see and be seen, each trying to outdo the other by the value of the gifts they brought. The Kings' many fans had also sent presents, and the opening of these provided great entertainment. Several hundred hand-knitted matinee jackets in lurid pink caused hoots of laughter and derision as they were consigned to a bin marked " orphanage". Guests " oh ahed" at the mountain of cuddly animals, and feigned vomiting at the sight of gory coloured mass produced toys. So engrossed was everyone that no one noticed Beauty grab a teddy until she gave a piercing scream and held up her bleeding hands. On examination, it was discovered that the innocent looking bear was impregnated with dozens of sharp needles. Amongst all the heaps of mail a note turned up, full of vile invective and threatening harm to Beauty.

Now Mr and Mrs King, being rich and famous, were not unused to receiving hate mail, but it was usually filtered by their secretaries, and so they were appalled that this had slipped through and had actually harmed, albeit not seriously, their precious child. All night long they paced the floor, wondering what to do. By morning, a plan had been decided upon.

Two weeks later, in a blaze of publicity, the Kings set off on a trip to visit a guru in India. A week after that, in another blaze of publicity, it was announced that their baby had contracted an exotic disease and died. The TV showed pictures of the heart-broken parents scattering her ashes in the sacred Ganges.

In reality, Princess Beauty had never gone to India but had been secreted away in the back of beyond. A young woman, named Georgina, had been discreetly engaged to care for her, and a small homestead was purchased for them in Montana. The people of nearby Smallsville did not suspect the strangers in the mountains of having Hollywood connections. Georgina told them that she had left a hectic life and an unfaithful husband in New York, to live a simple country life with her daughter, and they nodded approvingly.

Georgina's story was not completely untrue. She did indeed come from New York, where she had had a very unhappy childhood with a mouse of a mother and a pig of a father. She had married, at seventeen, a young man with a kind and gentle nature, but who was so laid back that he proved quite useless as a breadwinner, partner or handyman. Divorced at twenty-one, she married for the second time a young tiger in Wall Street, who worked all hours, made piles of money, and slept around. Divorced again at the age of twenty-four, Georgina's opinion of the male of the species was, to say the least, low. She enrolled on a university course, and graduated, summa cum laude, with a degree in Gender Studies, her opinions validated by scholarship. So when she was approached and offered a large sum of money and a secure future bringing up a female child (she was not told whose), she was glad to accept.

Georgie, as she preferred to be called, was determined to bring up Princess Beauty, now called Phoebe, as a thoroughly modern woman, never to be dependent on any male. They lived a very isolated but wholesome life, riding in the mountains, but never watching TV nor going to the movies. Georgie taught Phoebe at home, feeling fully confident of being able to pass on the benefits of her successful academic record. She also taught her to cook and sew, to mend fences, do basic plumbing and repair their pick-up truck. She warned her of the dangers of the world around them, which berries were poisonous, which plants would sting, and which four-legged critters were best avoided. But the most dangerous creature in the universe, Georgie repeatedly warned, walked not on four legs but two. And, according to Georgie, it kept all its brains, energies and drives between them. True, it could be charming and seductive, but it was all the more dangerous for that. It had only two aims towards her, and they were violence and domination.

And so time passed. Beauty grew up to live up to her name. She had long blonde hair, big blue eyes, and a sweet nature. She liked to sew pretty things for herself and Georgie liked to indulged her. For herself, however, Georgie found short cropped hair and dungarees far more practical.

For their eighteenth wedding anniversary, Arnie and Regina decided on a more select gathering than had been their wont in their younger days, and arranged an intimate dinner with their closest (read richest, most influential, film producer) friend and his wife, who coincidentally happened to have a son of marriageable age. The climax of the evening was when the Kings announced to their astonished guests that Princess Beauty was alive and well, and as beautiful a young woman as she had been a baby. They would not reveal her whereabouts but suggested how romantic it would be if Zak, their friend's son, could find her.

When the Peelburgs returned home, and put the proposition to their son, he found the challenge interesting. He had, after all, a Harvard education, (majoring in football) and hadn't anything particular to do that summer. St. Tropez was passé and Margueritte was full of drunken, geriatric plutocrats. Yes, he would take the challenge and prove the value of his expensive education.

It took Zak a full week of extensive research to find the best private detective in the land, and another two days to bribe him enough to drop all his other cases until he located Beauty. It took a month to track her down and reveal her whereabouts to Zak. (Actually, it only took him a week, but he span it out to ratchet up his expenses and to renew his acquaintance with his favourite places).

When Zak approached the little homestead in Montana, Georgie was in the field tending the horses while Beauty was dozing on a sunbed in the garden. Zak's heart missed a beat as he looked at her. She was indeed a beauty, and looked so sweet and innocent. On impulse, he knelt beside her, and gently and briefly kissed her lips. Phoebe opened her eyes and was immediately thrown into confusion. Here was one of the creatures against which Georgie had so often warned her, but he did not seem threatening. He was handsome, smiled broadly and said "Hi" cheerily. But then she remembered that Georgie had also told her of the guile and deviousness of the creature, and furthermore, he had touched her without permission. So she opened her mouth and screamed "Rape" at the top of her voice. Zak was so taken aback that before he had time to respond, Georgie had come running and knocked him clean out with a spade. When he awoke, he was in a police cell.

Smallsville, Montana, had heard of the expression "media circus" but never, up to that moment, truly understood the meaning. The recent events had furnished the international media with two momentous stories, the discovery of the Kings' daughter, and the alleged rape of her by the son of the most famous movie mogul in the world. They had to admit it was better than any story they'd ever made up. At the same time, a small army of women (all of them looking just like Georgie) arrived carrying banners and demanding dire punishment (involving surgery) for Zak, and indeed all males. At first, the people of Smallsville were put out by the commotion, but soon learned to take it all in their stride – and to make themselves a small fortune serving the needs of so many people.

Poor Phoebe was utterly traumatised by it all. Not only had she been raped (so she believed), but now discovered that Georgie was not her mother, and that she was the child of rich and famous movie stars, not the simple country child she thought she was. All she could say when questioned was, " He raped me." The Kings were utterly devastated by this outcome of their best intended plans. Moreover, their relationship with the Peelburgs was ruined. Georgie was beside herself with guilt and angst, that, despite all her warnings, a male had violated her precious Phoebe. Zak vehemently, but with decreasing heart, protested his innocence, and would, had he had the vocabulary, have described his situation as Kafkaesque. His mother was hysterical. Amidst all this, only Stefan Peelburg kept his head. (After all, he was not the biggest movie mogul for nothing). He hired the best, the brightest lawyer in all America, and made sure that she was female.

Ms Smart was tall and elegant. Her hair was perfectly coiffed, her nails neatly filed and her Chanel suit creaseless. She was married to a company director, had six happy and well-adjusted children, an outstanding law degree from Yale, and a formidable reputation. In short, Ms Smart was a modern Superwoman. As such, she also possessed a good deal of nous and it did not take her long to get the measure of the situation. She had only to observe Georgie when she looked at a man, ANY man, to see the loathing in her eyes. Her subtle woman-to-woman probing of Georgie in the witness box soon revealed the latter's background and prejudices.

She surreptitiously observed Phoebe, and noticed that whenever she looked at Zak, it was with a mixture of confusion and even sympathy for his highly distressed state. As a mother, she gently, but skilfully questioned the child in the witness stand. Bit by bit, the full story and the nature of the misunderstanding emerged, to the gasps of those who listened.

Poor Beauty was traumatised yet again, when she understood the enormity of her accusation, and it took two years of work by a highly paid therapist before the damage was repaired. Zak forgave her completely, for it was clear that she was an innocent. Indeed, his heart went out to her, and he visited her often. Before long, Beauty found that she longed for the touch of his lips on hers, and, on her twenty-first birthday, they were quietly married. When their first child was born, Phoebe, as she preferred to be known, rejected any suggestions of nannies or housekeepers and opted to look after her son herself, making sure that he was well integrated into the local community.

Georgie went to live in a women's commune, where she found some happiness, and where Phoebe visited her occasionally. Ms Smart took her whole brood on a luxury trip to Europe with her $ 2,000,000 fee, where they had a wonderful time. Stefan Peelburg did not mind the $ 2,000,000. That was small change to him. He recouped it tenfold by turning the whole story into the biggest grossing movie of the decade.

Linda Thatcher

IX

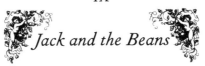

Jack and the Beans

"Where there's muck there's brass" OR "You gotta have a swine to find the truffles".

Edward Albee, *Who's afraid of Virginia Woolf?*

---

ack lived with his mam in a high rise flat in the West End of Newcastle. They had food on the table, a TV and a video but there is no doubt that they lived in what sociologists term "relative deprivation". There was never enough money to purchase the many and varied goods displayed nightly on TV and available in the many shops in the modern consumer society in which they lived. They got money from the Social of course and Jack's mam occasionally "entertained" gentlemen but there was never any chance of ends meeting. Jack's mam placed her hopes in her son. She bought him a football and a Newcastle United strip (at an exorbitant price) in the hope that he would become an overpaid soccer star. One Christmas she had spent her last few pounds on a second hand guitar convinced that Jack would become the next Noel Gallagher. Disappointingly, Jack showed no aptitude for either football or music. In desperation she even encouraged him to work hard at school – perhaps he would become a brain surgeon or space scientist and at least earn a liveable wage. But Jack preferred to sleep at school, it being rather noisy at night where he lived. He left school without taking his GCSEs, well prepared for a life on the dole.

That year, as Christmas approached, Jack's mam just could not find the money for Jack's £200 trainers, £100 sweatshirt and £55 baseball cap (designer of course) that he so desperately needed, not to mention the Christmas booze and food. So, with great reluctance, she took from a small envelope at the bottom of her drawer, her mother's wedding ring and gave it to Jack, instructing him to pawn it. "Don't take less than £20," she called after him.

Jack set out but when he got to the corner of the street he met a smart geezer in a sharp suit leaning on a flashy car. "Hey you, where you going?" he asked Jack. Jack told him. The guy put his arm round Jack and said, "Don't do that.

~ 31 ~

Give me the ring and I'll give you five magic beans which will end all your troubles." Gullible Jack agreed to the deal.

On the way home, Jack ate one of the beans and was immediately transported into a beautiful, wondrous world. Colours were vivid and glowing and he could not only see them but smell, feel, taste and touch them. Food tasted

SCUM 1

K. Hazeldine '17

"*The lad done good*"

like nothing he'd ever tasted before and the music he heard convinced him he'd never heard music before.

Some hours later, when the world had resumed its usual grey colour, Jack realised that he was in trouble. He had no money to take to his mam. However, he did have four magic beans left, so he detoured to the local disco where he sold them for £25 each. The next day Jack pawned the video for £100, bought magic beans, kept two for himself and sold the rest for £200. Jack had found his vocation at last.

In time, Jack learned to bypass the smart guy on the corner and was soon dealing big time with a couple of dozen runners working for him. Inevitably though, the smart guy had a boss, Mr Big, who was beginning to take exception to Jack's entrepreneurialism. He sent two of his biggest henchmen to fetch Jack to him, intending to give the boy a good talking to and a good going over.

He had Jack brought to him in a warehouse where he confronted him. He was an exceptionally tall and portly man and completely dwarfed poor Jack. He took a draw on his large cigar, savouring his power, and said menacingly,

> "Fe Fi Fo Fum, I smell the blood of a little piece of scum
> You've poached on my patch and stole my gold
> For you, my lad there'll be no growing old."

(He liked a touch of drama.) Jack merely eyed him coolly and then, before anyone had time to realise what was happening, he whipped a samurai sword from beneath his trench coat and shortened Mr Big by a head. "You work for me now," he told the henchmen. "Yes Sir, Mr. Jack," they quickly agreed.

Jack and his mam moved to a mansion in Ponteland. They also had a villa in Spain where they spent a month every winter but which could provide a more permanent home should it ever become necessary. Jack drives a Mercedes and wears Armani suits and acts as a role model for fatherless boys in the West End. His mam wears three gold and diamond rings on every digit, voluminous fur coats and drives a pink Cadillac convertible. (Well, money is no guarantee of good taste.) Whenever anyone asks about her son, she swells with pride and answers, "The lad done good."

Linda Thatcher

X

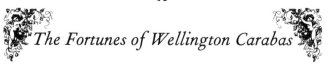

The Fortunes of Wellington Carabas

"There was a young lady of Riga".

Old Limerick

---

here was a mother of three sons, who was left a widow by her husband, a naturalised Portuguese. As a patriot he respected the long association of his country with England and named his youngest son after the hero who liberated Portugal from the oppression of that great dictator, Napoleon. Of course, that was a long time ago, but to patriots time only enriches history. He called his youngest son Wellington, to the disgust of his wife. When he died, his two elder sons had left home and already had young families. Wellington's mother regretted bitterly that she was left with this youngest son with his smooth feline looks. Not at all like his sturdy and practical brothers, with his huge slanting dark eyes, small features and pale skin. They often suggested that he was not properly male or words to that effect and had added to his problems with the rougher elements of the local village youth. Now they were away and there was just Wellington and his mam, and the black cat called Salamanca. There was no money to spare but Wellington was of an inventive mind and when he got to an age when he needed to make an impression with some gear, it was to his mother's dated wardrobe that he turned. He found a crystal necklace and earrings, a pale blue lace blouse, black ski pants and a quilted waistcoat. What was he like! A pair of size seven derry boots from Oxfam completed the image of a river dancer which he enhanced by a mouth-organ. This last he carried around, constantly blowing. His other constant was Salamanca who followed him everwhere. He cut a figure all right. His attractive looks drew favourable attention from the local girls who likened him to two very successful performers of popular music but he returned no interest. His only desire was to equal his brothers in the eyes of his mother and prove to be full of unexpected talent. He had always fancied himself as a great performer and was sure that one day he would make his mark. And he had a hero's name to conjure with, unlike his brothers Dick and Harry.

One day in the drinking place he was used to frequent, where he sipped his

Wellington sets off on the road to Waterloo but history will not repeat itself.

coke and Salamanca got a dish of milk, he was playing sentimental tunes on his harmonica as usual. The evening wore on, and two men came in whose style of dressing was not too dissimilar to his own. They sat quietly together and well on in the evening approached him to play some requests. They questioned him afterwards about his circumstances and said they could promise him better. They gave him a card with a phone number which indicated an agency of some sort, and left. Wellington recognised the call when it came. As he told his mother next morning, the world was out there and so was his fortune. She was not sorry to see him go as she could not imagine what use he was ever going to be. He had also taken to borrowing her makeup, and she had found some interesting underwear at the back of his drawer.

Wellington left to follow up the invitation of the human prospectors at an address in the Capital many miles away. Borrowing his mother's fake ocelot coat, (he did not worry her by telling her and, as it was summer, he did not expect it would be missed for a while), he took himself to the motorway roundabout where he sat down to play his mouthorgan while he waited for a lift. Salamanca sat watchful at his side. The lorry driver who stopped expressed keen disappointment that the payment was in the form of a rendering of "Sailing" that was entirely musical and Wellington had to leave that lift sooner than he had hoped. The next was in a Daimler and the softly spoken driver took him all the way and proffered his card should he ever be embarrassed about accommodation.

"There's something here I'm not getting," thought Wellington. Coming to the address the men had given him, Wellington was faced with a huge tower block. On the seventeenth floor, he was welcomed by one of the men who congratulated him on his decision. They had plans for him. More of them later. He had no objection to staying with them ? They were not interfering with any of his private arrangements? Good. Then it's all settled. There were piano lessons. Visits to hairdressers and gear shops. No great change in style but much in quality and expense. The plan as revealed matched him with a baby grand, candelabras and his Salamanca, who would accompany him everywhere and be his stage mascot.

The promoters were not wrong. They had turned up a winner. Two years on and Wellington Carabas was a household name with the teenies and especially beloved of ladies of a certain age. His silk purple shirts, diamonds, snakeskin boots, his huge fake fur coats and customised cars with chauffeur in tight blue velvet suit, were always good for a photograph. Salamanca was replaced by a bigger sort of cat called Rodrigo for short, who was in turn replaced by an even bigger sort called Badajoz until his image and reputation were sealed for all time in mythology by a tiger called Waterloo that lay at his feet on stage and accompanied him everywhere else, on a jewelled chain. The shekels jingled in. The ivories tinkled out in tunes reminiscent of the forties and fifties. And to complete the image, the mother of Wellington, who had struggled so hard to give her orphaned fatherless son nothing but the best, now was brought forth to praise the best son in the world as she posed outside the large detached house, the new Astra she had yet to learn to drive, etcetera. She did not mention the coat. The brothers did refuse his offer, through his agents, of financial help with a repetition of remarks such as they were wont to make. These did not go down well with their offspring, who were proud of their connection with such a famous uncle.

Where would it all end? The end nearly came with a scabrous newspaper which libelled his tiger as an abused animal. It had nothing to gain but publicity and nothing to lose but more. The tiger could not give evidence and the matter was settled out of court but some animal rights people got hold of it all and staged unpleasant scenes with placards outside stagedoors where he performed.

Some time later, people were reminded of this when Wellington Carabas came to a dramatic and mysterious end. Not appearing in time for a stage rehearsal, his managers were called to his accommodation in the penthouse of the Astorias to find the Waterloo lolling as usual on the silk sheets of the bed, and no sign then or ever of Wellington Carabas except for his snakeskin and diamond boots.

When asked for her comment, his mother referred to his father's choice of his name, his use of her clothes, the theft of her coat, and the fact that he had only ever really loved the cat.

_____

Margaret Whyte

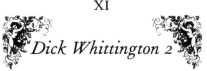

XI

Dick Whittington 2

"O Fortuna velut luna".

Carmina Burana

Once a poor abused boy called Dick ran away from his neglectful and cruel parents to join others like him in Cardboard City. He soon learned how to do, sitting on old bits of matting with "Hungry and Homeless" written on a broken board in front of him. One night a starving kitten crawled into his rat's nest of a doss and he kept it for its warmth. It ate what he did. One day, after it had grown into a marmalade Tom and was sitting as usual by him, a loose pitbull bit Dick and chased the cat. Only after he had located Tom, was Dick taken to hospital, where he was treated and his cat given milk by kindly nurses. Back on the street, Tom took to growling whenever he saw a dog and one day Dick could hardly believe his ears when he thought he heard his cat say words to the effect of "go away dog." He asked his mate, with whom he shared the night watches against pickpockets and worse, if he had heard right but there was no doubt that the cat's speech was getting clearer all the time. It did not just urge dogs to leave but started asking Dick for a sip of his tea and "giss a chip" in its sibilant growl.

Dick got his mates to bring dogs and stand in front of him and the fame of the talking cat spread as Dick's takings rocketed. The police became more sympathetic even though groups grew into crowds on the street and sure enough a television crew materialised to film the tramp with the cat. They were soon on TV on programmes of wonderful and strange pets, starting with Esther Rantzen and progressing to animal behaviourists. Tom made Dick's fortune. He moved off the street into a bedsit, for security. He was contacted by an Agency offering to get bookings in return for fees and conditions such as Tom being minded against the possibility of kidnap, and receiving a course of injections against catflu.

As you may expect, no good came of all this. The Agency was contacted by an unpleasant character who claimed the cat was his and he had been searching

for it ever since it disappeared as a kitten. He really just wanted to be paid off for trying it on but Dick got a shock and threatened him with a visit from some of his mates who were not on the "hungry and homeless". The newspapers got interested in the developments of the story and the Agency persuaded Dick to sell exclusive rights to the *Sun*. Amidst all this the cat disappeared. The Agency instituted proceedings against Dick for breach of contract and not observing the terms of the agreement to safeguard the cat. Dick was distraught and back on the streets alone, for no one, not even any of his former mates, was interested in him now. The publicity died down as suddenly as it had all erupted. Dick felt very depressed. The police chased him when they saw him. He did badly in his daily collections. Former admirers accused him and the cat of cheating.

Just when Dick was thinking of ending it all the cat reappeared in his doss, looking very sleek. It sat looking at him with a strange smile on its face. Encouraging? Suddenly it pounced onto the pavement and stalked off with its tail erect. Dick followed hopefully. The cat walked for hours, never looking back, until they arrived at the river at a place called Strand-on-Green. There the cat turned into a wide driveway screened by box and yew. It sat, with its tail curled round and its head high, on the patterned marble veranda in front of a huge door with a multi-coloured glass fanlight. Dick dared not approach the doorway and kept calling the cat to him. It ignored him but a young girl came out and let the cat in. "Hey," said Dick. "That's my cat." The girl took one look at him and went in fast and shut the door. Dick was exhausted from his unaccustomed exertion and fell sideways into the box hedge. Two men approached from the back of the house and spoke into the bushes where his boots were all that was visible, and told him to leave. "Not without my cat what talks. It's my cat in there, been on Telly and everything," said Dick. "You've pinched it." At this the men offered physical encouragement to assist Dick to leave. In his state of fatigue and despair Dick wept and droned over and over as he drummed his feet in the hedge. "It's my cat it's my cat it's my cat I'm not going without it," or words to that effect. The girl and a very tall man stood in the porch to see the commotion as he was hauled out. They saw a dirty tramp, very thin with a white exhausted face now tearstained. "You've got all this, give me my cat, it's all I got." he was going on.

Well the girl's father who worked in the City indulged his daughter's pleas for the cat and the tramp both to stay. Now that Dick was ensconced on a futon in the loft above the stables, the cat talked again. Mr Adman had his reward with a very hot property and knew exactly how to insure and market it with a large advertising firm that brought Dick a substantial income while he had a place in the household learning the skills of living as others did. Dick's stories of abuse went down well with the dinner guests he served and the City family were pleased to have personal contact with the "real" world in the form of an abused ex-tramp.

Dick was sent on day release to College, did well in Hotel and Catering, invested his cat money which by now was considerable, augmented by merchandising and by many Sons of Tom and all the cat cult figures. He continued to live in the loft until the City Man had a serious talk about his investments and prospects. There was a bit of discomfort in the City family when Dick took Tom's advice about the daughter and small Dicks etcetera but that panned out too and they are all living happily with the talking Tom and some of his offspring who have inherited the right genes which Mr. Adman has advised Dick to have cloned. So there it is.

Margaret Whyte

...the head of state
in the clouds ...

XII

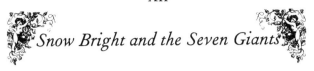
Snow Bright and the Seven Giants

> "You can fool all the people some of the time,
> and some of the people all the time
> but you cannot fool all the people all the time."
>
> Attrib. Abraham Lincoln

ot so long ago, in a land not so far away, there lived a young queen much loved by her people. This was just as well for the queen dwelt in a wondrous palace which floated high above the realm on a fluffy pink cloud made up entirely of her people's adoration. The whole of the queen's attention was upon the condition of the cloud, for it was known to her that in other realms where monarchs had incurred their people's displeasure, their clouds had vanished into nothingness, their palaces had crashed to the ground and the monarchs had lain lifeless among the debris.

The queen worked hard to ensure her popularity. She married a handsome prince and produced four healthy children, three of them boys. She regally opened Parliaments, graciously snipped ribbons declaring roads, bridges etc. open. She imperiously visited foreign lands, extolling the virtues of her country's products and condescendingly allowed the people occasional glimpses of her and her family.

Despite her hard work, the queen was always anxious regarding the state of the cloud, so she sent for her most trusted adviser. He procured for her a device which hung on the wall and looked for most of the time like a mirror. However, underneath it was a button and the adviser told the queen to say the words

"Tell me, tell me, magic screen,
Am I still the most adored queen?"

at 6:00 p m. or 10:00 p. m. and then press the button. When the queen did this, the blank screen jumped into life and a face appeared which told her:

"Indeed, indeed your majesty
No one in the land is as adored as thee."

This reassured the queen greatly and every evening without fail she consulted the screen.

For many years all was well. The land prospered and the palace floated securely on the pink fluffy cloud. Then, one fateful day, the queen noticed that the cloud was not as buoyant as it had been. In a state of dread, she waited for 6:00 p. m. Her heart almost stopped when she heard the screen's message:

"Beware O queen. Watch out, watch out.
A dreadful beast is loose about.
His name, his name is Monoxout."

All night the queen tossed and turned wondering what to do. Next morning she consulted her elder statesmen, who said, "Perhaps, ma'am, you should go among the people more." This idea was so repugnant to the queen that her husband offered to go in her stead. Unfortunately, try as he might, he was quite unable to disguise his disgust at the commoners and had to be hastily recalled. What could be done? It so happened that the queen's daughter was sporty, good enough in fact to be chosen for the national team. Surely this would restore the royal family's prestige. Unfortunately, when the people tried to take the princess's photograph, she told them resoundingly to "Sod off."

Little by little the cloud was evaporating and every night the screen said ominously:

"Monoxout is thriving and well.
Pay heed, oh queen, to the tolling of the bell."

The queen was in despair and called her eldest son Prince Charmless (known as Chas to his friends). "Oh my poor son," she cried, "I fear you may never be King." As she dabbed the tears from her eyes, she gave a sudden start. He was a lot bigger than she remembered. (Busy queens don't have much time for bringing up children). "How old are you?" she demanded. "Almost thirty," he replied. The queen began to cry again. This time with joy. "We're saved," she sobbed. "You must marry. Find a sweet (and virgin) princess. We'll have a huge wedding, all pomp and ceremony. The people will love us again."

Finding a princess to fit the requirements was not easy as most of the prince's contemporaries were too old to be either sweet or virgin. Eventually someone remembered the younger sister of one of the prince's former girlfriends and she was duly produced for the queen to examine. She seemed perfect. Just eighteen, she smiled sweetly up at the queen from under her fringe. She was clean and fresh and pure as the driven snow and consequently was called Snow

Bright, although her friends called her Bri. She fell headlong in love with Chas and as for him, he had been brought up to do his duty.

The wedding was the talk of the whole world. The social occasion of the century. In quick succession, two baby boys were born and the queen could sleep peacefully at night, knowing that the cloud was pinker and fluffier than ever.

This continued for several years until once again the queen detected that the cloud was fading. Once again she turned anxiously to her screen for news although she was dreading what she would hear.

"Beware the ticking of the monarchy's clocks.
Chas and Bri's marriage is on the rocks."

The queen almost fainted with shock but worse was to come. The next night the queen was confronted by a picture of Bri speaking to the people, saying:

"I'm as wronged as wronged as wronged as can be
Because of my husband's gross infidelity."

The next night was even more shocking. A picture of Chas appeared and said:

"It's true I sought solace in the arms of another
Bri's bulimic, bad-tempered and not much of a lover."

The queen was appalled. She summoned Chas and Bri to the palace to remind them of their duty, but no amount of pleading, commanding or remonstrating could reconcile them. And when she switched on the screen it said ominously,

"The monarchy's name is blacker than mud,
But Monoxout is seen as all good."

The queen was in a quandary. What was she to do? She was pretty fed up with Chas but, in the final analysis, blood is thicker than water, so she called her trusted henchman and commanded him, "Get rid of Princess Bri. Thrust her into the wilderness. She is no longer royal."

Poor Snow Bright , so pretty, so wronged but, unfortunately for the queen, no longer so sweet or so naive. She had rather liked being royal. She too had felt the people's adoration and longed for it more and more. "I know," she thought to herself, "I'll make myself Queen of People's Hearts." She made her way to a huge mansion where, she knew, lived the mighty giant, Mediaman.

He welcomed her with open arms and said, "Don't worry. I have six stalwart brothers. We'll look after you and restore you to your rightful place." And he introduced her to them. First was Fashion. He was suave and elegant and Snow Bright was much admired when out and about with him. Four of the brothers were deformed and ugly but aroused the people's sympathy. They were named Aids, Famine, Landmine and Sickness. That the beautiful and regal Snow Bright showed them such kindness raised her standing enormously. The last brother was just a child but with him Snow Bright was always such fun and so motherly.

Back at the palace, the queen consulted the screen with a growing sense of helplessness. She was all too aware of the precariousness of her position. Each night the news was worse, until at last the screen pronounced:

"Monoxout's star grows brighter and brighter
But your cloud gets ever weaker and lighter."

Two days later the cloud finally disappeared. The palace fell to the ground with an almighty crash and shattered into a thousand pieces. The queen, Prince Charmless and all the royal family lay lifeless among the ruins. Princess Bri permitted herself a slight smile. After all they'd got no more than they deserved, hadn't they? She rushed over to Mediaman's house. "Now I'll be Queen!" she exclaimed. Mediaman gave her a pitying glance. "Sorry, baby. Monarchs are out. Must dash! Got a president to interview!"

" In that case," said Snow Bright, " you'd better introduce us. The sooner the better."

Sadly, this was not to be the last twist in the story of the bright princess.

Linda Thatcher

XIII

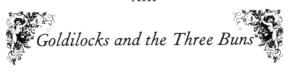

Goldilocks and the Three Buns

"Be not weary in well doing."

Paul, *Thessalonicans 2, 3, xiii*

---

nce upon a time in Barnard Castle, a gluttonous girl who was as butter-fat as her golden curls went for a walk. It was a beautiful Saturday morning in May . . . and "I'm hungry," thought Goldilocks. She had already wolfed three bowls of porridge for her breakfast that morning, much to the alarm of her mother. Her parents were quietly considering referring Goldilocks for counselling. She appeared to be developing a compulsive obsession with the number three. She always ate three of everything (except for small things, like peas). When asked, for instance, to tidy her

A bun too far . . . .

K. Hageldine '97

room, she would always reply by saying "s. d off," or something similar, three times.

Having stopped at the bakery for three muesli slices and three pizza slices, Goldilocks bore her picnic off to the castle grounds. Lots of people were there enjoying the sunshine. Goldilocks sat down on a bench. Nearby, a man and woman were playing "throw the beanbag" with their small son. Goldilock's picnic soon vanished as she watched them. Gradually, and with increasing intensity, her narrow blue gaze focused on their hamper nearby.

Ten minutes later the family sat down for their lunch. "But where is my Chelsea bun?" asked Mr Bear in surprise. "And where has my iced bun gone to?" inquired Mrs Bear. "My bun has gone too," wailed little Bear, "and look, that fat girl is eating it !" It was true. Her jaws were working as hard as ever they could, but there was incriminating evidence in the guilty hands of Goldilocks, and in the devoted presence of several pigeons.

The outraged Bears made a dash for her demanding an explanation and reparation and in consternation, she fled. Mr Bear had only last week had his car broken into, and he was feeling a bit sensitive on issues of petty crime and justice. He gave chase down Horsemarket. Of course, he soon caught up with her, accepting the fact that he was making a public spectacle of himself, in his determination that Right was Might.

And then, her three bowls of porridge, her three muesli slices, the three pizza slices, and of course, the three buns, overwhelmed Goldilocks. It was extremely jarring to have had the final bun interrupted, a trinity broken. The unaccustomed physical exertion was the last straw.

"Why don't you **** off, you tosser, tosser, TOSSER!" she enunciated and was sick once, twice, and finally, thrice, upon his new beige Hush Puppies. The shoelaces were never the same.

Soon afterwards, her parents referred her for psychotherapy with a most caring practitioner. It was the severest reprisal they could devise.

K-E Hazeldine

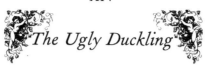

XIV

The Ugly Duckling

"One is never as unhappy as one thinks, nor as happy as one hopes".

La Rochefoucauld

 successful and stunning woman adopted a baby girl whom she dressed and presented beautifully, but, try as she might, no one ever called the child beautiful. The baby turned out to have what is known as a lazy eye which would need obscuring with a patch to correct. As she grew older it became clear that serious orthodontics would be called for. As she grew older still her nose and jaw were rather near. In adolescence much deviation from classical proportions could be noted in a narrow flat chest and a comfortable bottom. If the daughter was dissatisfied with her appearance relative to her mother, the reverse was also true. Fortunately, the mother had means at her disposal and when it was obvious that this duck needed assistance to become a swan, the mother's chequebook was at the ready. What the mother started, the daughter continued to build on with nose bob, eyebrow shaping, chin reduction, breast implants, tucks here, there and everywhere. This was made possible with the estate of her adoptive mother who died at the height of worldly success at the wheel of her Jaguar.

The daughter moved far away to where no one knew her and bought into a cosmetic surgery business to recoup in profits what she had spent in pursuit of her ideal. The company prospered. She took advantage of the complete menu of treatments on the house and finally married the Svengali whose skills had created a face and body to compete with other rich businesswomen, if not exactly to die for. A daughter was born who looked a lot like her mother at the age when no one could now remember her. Her mother was very disappointed in her daughter's appearance and planned with her husband how soon they could start on the task of liberating the butterfly from this unsightly chrysalis. Indeed her mother had forgotten any appearance she had sported midway between nature and nurture.

As the child grew, however, she expressed no problem with her appearance and the bandaged mummies she had grown up amongst filled her with amaze-

The duck looks into the pond

KC Hazeldine '97

ment that people should want to make themselves ill. You can tell from this that this child is her own person. She continued to grow less than beautiful but lively, clever and charming. Her bright eyes with a slight squint gleamed behind the horn rims she preferred to contact lenses. She refused to wear her braces over her large yellowish teeth which were revealed in all their glory as she laughed loud and often. Her flat chest always sported some urgent exhortation to save world, dolphins, forests, or whatever. Her big round bottom shook under her voluminous layers of ethnic skirts. To her mother's anxious enquiries as to her reactions to her appearance, she replied tranquilly that she had the best parents and a good education. The house was always full of her friends with whom she was always planning some committed activity. Was there anything wrong with her that she was not aware of? "No, no," said her mother hastily. "Nothing at all." "We can't all be beautiful like you mummy. One in the family is enough. "

One rainy day, while rummaging about for some gear in the loft, she spied a dusty brown box that looked as if it had not been touched for years. The straps fell off as she touched them. Inside were old envelopes full of papers and at the bottom, in a wallet, she found her mother's adoption papers and some photographs of a well dressed but unprepossessing child to whom she thought she bore a resemblance. Spreading all the contents of the box over the floor she followed the stages of her mother's transformation, recorded in the photographs, taken with and without her beautiful adoptive mother.

"Oh my poor mother, to have gone through all that. How disappointed she must have been in me. Now I understand how concerned my mother has been about me. I must have been blind to be so unaware and ungrateful as not to take advantage of her offers of help. No doubt every other daughter would have been glad of so generous a mother. I'll accept her offer when next she asks me. I have been very selfish going around looking as I do and not thinking I am an eyesore to others."

She spoke about what she had found and what she had decided as a consequence to her current boyfriend, who was finishing his doctorate on the breeding habit of a species of sea urchin which lives on the scraps of what captive red salmon eat as they live their lives in plastic pens in the sea lochs. He was horrified. "How could you think of going around so unnatural and not yourself!" he exclaimed. "What are you thinking about?" "What is natural?" she retorted, "and what do you think you are working on? And don't you think

I owe something to my parents who have brought me up so generously? And what about family loyalty? I have no choice."

"At least leave it till you have completed your studies," he urged. "No," she said. "If I do I shall lose my nerve. I've made my mind up."

Sadly her boyfriend left. She joined the other world of those who will not accept the hand of fate, the movers and shakers of the world, and in time took over the chairmanship of the company from her very proud mother who welcomed her into the family tradition, for it is not nothing to turn ducks – or is it geese – into swans.

Margaret Whyte

XV

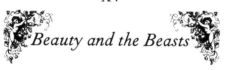

Beauty and the Beasts

"Hypocrisy is the homage paid by vice to virtue."

La Rochefoucauld, *Maximes*, 218

---

here was once an extraordinarily beautiful girl whose very correct parents never failed to remind her that beauty was not only skin deep, but also unfair, and could cause considerable problems for the possessor. Beauty did have problems at school from jealous classmates who objected to the way she was always picked on to be Mary in the Christmas plays, given other leading roles in school events, and, later, always the recipient of the most Valentine cards as expression of male admiration. Indeed, she had a mixed time at school, from both teachers and pupils, despite a lovely nature and an excellent attitude to study.

She was also cursed with a keen intelligence and a strong sense of duty, both of which natural handicaps gave her further unfair advantages when she entered the world of work as a trainee accountant, after gaining a first class honours degree. Her parents never stopped reminding her of the need to be wary of her so-called good fortune and the competition from others equally deserving, but less charming. Beauty had lived since early childhood in a state of increasing guilt. She had acquired camouflage to disguise her looks and her intelligence by insignificant clothes and a deeply reticent manner. Her depth and quality of conscience and kindness could not be so easily hidden and Beauty had also been burdened from an early age by the claims of rejects and misfits of all types, who sensed in her a victim of their repressed and distorted needs. She was never free from the attentions of the office creep, or the need for emotional female company from young men with serious physical challenges. She accepted to go out with two very large girls from the computing section who recognised her pulling power under her disguises. She was a soft touch for flag days and fund raising activities for charities.

Ever since her early teens, many handsome and successful young men had asked her out, but because she saw they were attractive and desired openly by other girls, she sadly and gently refused them. She still lived at home with her

parents who perpetually warned her of her unfair and undeserved advantages. One day, in despair, she considered specifically what she could do to break out of her trap. She always understood that missionaries and social workers were a truly superior class of persons with whom she could not be compared.

One day a new trainee appeared in the office. He was less than five feet tall, had bright red hair which grew in strange clumps out of a very large head, and what can only be described as a humped back. She heard his booming voice before she saw him. At coffee, he made a beeline for her and chatted away with great aplomb about his parents who lived in Brighton and his university years at Sussex and how he applied for and got this traineeship. Afterwards, one of the undermanagers who had unsuccessfully petitioned Beauty, implied that the new trainee was chosen to make some contribution to the firm's need to employ so many people who were challenged in some way, who in this case fitted the bill at no extra expense except a new adjustable desk chair.

As Beauty agreed to accompany him to his model train club and orchestral concerts, she felt secure from the claims of envy. Heads turned all right as they passed, but with other expressions. Her companion's apparent unawareness of the challenge he posed to others, and seeming acceptance of her disguise, half convinced Beauty that she had been right to heed her parents. When he hinted at a suggestion of marriage, she offered directly to marry him as soon as possible and stood up against the horrified response of her parents, defending the logic of her position as emphasised by them for as long as she could remember. On her wedding day she was astonished at the virulence of the comments from some senior lady spectators as she left the church. She felt reassured, however, in the worth of her husband below the skin, and secure in her attempts to right the wrong of her attraction. Whenever they appeared in public together, she had reason to be convinced of the weight of her penance. At work, they were ostracised by embarrassed colleagues. For Beauty this was a liberation. At last she could afford to show her natural advantages because they only emphasised her commitment to making good the unfairness of nature. She let her expenditure soar on clothes, makeup and all kinds of beauty products including perfumes, which filled the offices with luxury and sensuality. Her husband was beside himself with pride and joy, such as made young men violent in their thoughts and imaginative in their speculations about what they would like to do to him. Public abuse followed them wherever they went. On one occasion, they were refused a hotel room on the grounds that she must be on a professional assignment and no way would they accept this was her husband.

She passed her qualifying exams first time. Her husband did not. He blamed her for his failure as she was causing him so much more aggression than he had encountered before. Beauty was devastated by his reaction and sought comfort from her two fat friends who gave her a mouthful instead. She consulted her mother who roundly abused her for bringing degradation on the family. She was horrified to learn in this way of how deep beauty or its absence went in the eyes of her parent. Beauty had a lot of thinking to do.

She decided to do it well away from everything and everybody and, scanning the holiday brochures for a place in the sun, saw evidence that there she may expect to find others of comparable if not equal beauty, but, from their postures, no guilt at all and, from their companions as photographed, an expectation of equal beauty in their partners. "Perhaps they see things differently there," she thought to herself, and booked a fortnight's holiday in Barbados to be taken during a dismal London February.

On the plane she was eyed up by a very beautiful young man of colour who was visiting his family still living in Barbados. He was a lawyer specialising in land deals whose family welcomed her warmly. His colour was very attractive to her and she wondered if the depth of his appearance was any different from that of her husband. She determined to find out on their return to London by moving out from her marital home into that of the black lawyer. Reaction back at work was favourable to the news that she had left her husband and people felt free to say all sorts of unacceptable things, which, they told her, they had wanted to say before. A very careful silence followed the revelation, some weeks later, of her new arrangements. Not from her parents, however, who seemed at this point very convinced of the seriousness of the depth of the skin unless related to beauty. "But he is very beautiful," Beauty reassured them, "so there is no need to worry."

They remained unconvinced. She had done the wrong thing again. Not at work though. Her presence, speed of working, accuracy and grasp of detail brought rapid promotion. Shortly after her return from the Caribbean, her husband disappeared from view, presumably back to Brighton. The black lawyer found her parents too much to stomach and went off to fry his own fish and Beauty felt again the reactions of the world at large to her extraordinary looks. She had long blown her camouflage. When the recently widowed Managing Director asked her to dinner in a legendary restaurant, she accepted and during the fifth course (Devils on Horseback), she asked for his opinion on the curse of beauty. He invited her to move in with him and find out. She accepted. He was not beautiful but he was very deep. And rich. Her parents approved. She did not care if they did or not. For a bright girl, some might have said that she was a bit slow in arriving at a conclusion about who were the biggest beasts in her life and they were certainly more than skin deep. Deeply beastly.

Margaret Whyte

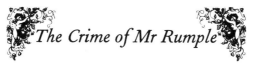

XVI

The Crime of Mr Rumple

"Hope deferred maketh the heart sick."

Proverbs 13, xii

---

 ow that I am in my fifties, with four grown-up children, all of whom seem to be producing grandchildren at the moment, I feel that I have much to be grateful for. Fate has been kind to me. I am surrounded by people I care for. I am healthy, touch wood. I have a little money. I have a face that is agreeable to look at. This last thing reflects no credit upon me but I am everlastingly thankful for it.

My oldest brother is dead now, bless him. As a baby he had an adventure which terrified our parents, rocked the neighbourhood and provided sensational fodder for the national newspapers. A funny and extraordinarily ugly little man kidnapped him and was sent to prison for it.

My mother had wheeled William to the shops in his pram one morning. She parked him outside the butcher's but she almost immediately noticed a neatly dressed but hideous looking little man peering into the pram. She flurried out. She could hear the man making little cooing noises. She elbowed him aside. "Excuse me," she said smartly, and she came straight home, quivering with aftershock.

Later she told herself that she had been silly. People were always making a fuss of the baby. It was entirely natural. But the man's face and body were so twisted. His face was so yellow. His expression, so briefly seen, was startled of course but also, what word conveyed it, . . . well, hungry. Just like Dad used to look when confronted with his favourite bangers in onion gravy. (This was how my mother described it to me, years later.)

On fine days she would tuck William up and wheel him into the small garden while she did the washing. She could watch him through the window. One morning the telephone rang and she went to answer it. When she picked up the receiver, the caller hung up. When she returned to the kitchen and glanced through the window, the perambulator was not there. William had gone.

Imagine the sudden mental blankness, the sense of disorientation, the

The handkerchief was not up to the job......

K.E Hazeldine 1997

gradual verbal articulation of the thought, "My baby has gone!" The scream that announces the realisation.

Mother dashed out into the road, looked left, looked right, nothing to be seen. Phone calls to the police, to my Dad's workplace, frantic knockings on neighbours' doors, interrogations of passersby. Cups of tea laced with whisky. The fear of murder hung in the air unsaid.

William was missing for four days until the police in the next town received a tip-off from a milkman who had a suspicious new customer. "We want two pints daily from now on. Full cream, please," said the customer. The milkman could see a perambulator in the hall. The man was known to be a bachelor. Small wonder, with such a frightful mug on him.

A surveillance operation was instigated, followed by a raid and a dramatic arrest. The trial was a nine-days wonder as the details emerged. It was discovered that the kidnapping Mr Rumple was actually a qualified solicitor, but working as a solicitor's clerk, trying to live as invisibly as possible.

In his house were no fewer than five cages of immaculately kept white mice. His kitchen was likewise clean and tidy, but there were rows of uneaten homebaked pies resting on a starched tablecloth. "Very tasty too, especially the ham and leek," remarked Constable Thomas. (This contribution was not entered in the records.)

William was lying in a crib absolutely festooned with hand-sewn muslin frills and giant blue bows.

When the police burst in Mr Rumple clutched William to him. William stared at him with serious ten-month-old eyes. William did not cry until Mr Rumple began to shout in a quivering voice, "Don't take him from me, oh don't take him away. I've got nobody, nobody, you've all got somebody, why shouldn't I have somebody, why can't I keep him, he is so lovely!"

When he was cornered and William removed from him, Mr Rumple was heard to wail, every bit as loudly as my mother had been heard to do, "I want the baby, give me back the baby!"

"I put the handcuffs on him as quick as you like," said Constable Harris to my mother later, over a cup of tea. Constable Harris was a great favourite with the local wives. He was married, and the father of young children too. "Yes," he went on, "it sounds strange, and I hope you won't mind me saying, but he gave me shivers down me spine and a lump in me throat all at the same time. I've not felt like that at an arrest before, but all them blue bows did something to me."

Mr Rumple looked even uglier, apparently, weeping loudly in court without a sufficiently large handkerchief. He had not expressed remorse for his crime, but the gallery audience excitedly agreed later that he had escaped with a remarkably light sentence, considering that he was a deranged monster, not safe to be let loose on the streets. They blamed his employer who had gone into the witness box to speak up for the accused.

"He's worked for me for twelve years. Highly competent. Thoroughly decent . . ."

In time, my mother forgave Mr Rumple, though my father never did. I have Mr Rumple to blame for my strictly supervised childhood. Our parents could hardly bear to let their children out of sight after that. But I can hardly count my blessings, and not spare a thought for Mr Rumple, now can I?

K-E Hazeldine

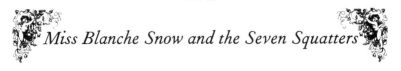

XVII

Miss Blanche Snow and the Seven Squatters

J'Accuse.

Emile Zola. *Open Letter on the Dreyfus Case 1898.*

O nce there was an outstandingly attractive lady who married a very quiet and pleasant man much older than herself, name of Mr Snow. Within a year she had a little girl called Blanche and realised that she had married into a very quiet bed indeed, despite the effect of her attractions which she had rather taken for granted. As her husband was such a nice man and a good husband in other ways and a most devoted father, she remained sufficiently contented with her lot for a number of years. Unfortunately, she did not realise that one must worship all the gods and any who are neglected will exact their revenge. Hers came in the form of a determined and handsome racing car driver she met at the sports car rallies she attended with her husband. He seemed to find the addition of her delightful little daughter an added bonus. He courted the lady boldly and openly and her courteous husband gave her the choice and promised a civilised arrangement should it go against him.

Braving the disapproval of friends, family and her daughter's school, she opted for life in the fast track. Her husband moved out of the family home so that his daughter should be disturbed as little as possible and young Lochinvar moved in. For a few years life was lived on a high and the lady took pride in her beautiful lover and her beautiful daughter now growing up fast. The fact that these two might eventually take great pride in each other and enjoy the risk of living dangerously in other ways did not occur to her, until her daughter confided in her best friend at school, who confided it to her mother, who confided it to her teacher, who confided it to the Social Services who paid a visit to the home. She and her unofficial stepfather-in-crime brazened it out but although the mother covered up for them she could no longer fool herself about what had been happening. She looked long, closely and carefully in the mirror. She looked long, closely and carefully at her daughter that evening. Her lover did not return to the home that day nor the next. The ensuing conversation with her daughter revealed that the daughter considered that she had every

right to the same illicit fruit her mother tasted. There were unedifying refer-
ences to pots and kettles. The mother found herself confronted by a younger,
more beautiful and less inhibited rival whose milk teeth had been cut, so to
speak, on coping with her mother's irregular situation.

The following day the school phoned to ask whether her daughter was ill as
she had not turned up. The father, the police, and the social services turned up
for the hunt. All to no avail. The lover telephoned to say he had now withdrawn
from the situation into an apartment of his own, and though he was promptly
visited by the searching parties and spent two days in residence helping the
police, it was established that he too knew nothing. The girl had vanished.
There were no leads.

In fact, there was someone who knew where she had gone. One of her more
discreet schoolfriends had a brother who had a band and lived in a squat, in
London. She gave Blanche Snow the address, promised secrecy and saw her
off at the station. As well as the friend's brother, there were six other squatters,
members of the band, in this lovely high ceilinged old house where they had
lived, undisturbed for some years now, as a well-integrated group. They were

all males but made no bones about finding her a place to put a mattress when she acquired one. She was given a list of her chores. She was quite surprised to find that they all had a paid job as well as playing in the band. They said she could do some of their duties in the house until she got some work.

She liked all except one who was very grumpy because he worked on the buses and had to get up very early to receive his daily round of abuse from the dissatisfied public. She became especially fond of one who had sticky out ears and could not read. He worked in a day care centre for old people. He loved the old people for their stories and they loved him for the pleasure he took in being useful to them. Another had a bad chest and always seemed to have a cold which he had been hoping for years that his job as a postman in the open air would clear up. Alas not! There was a black one who worked on the civic amenities lorries whose appalling stories of his findings, related with a huge white smile, kept them in stitches. Another worked as a hospital porter on permanent nights and she never saw him awake for he came and went in hours of darkness. He was black too. Another she hardly saw either. He was a computer software designer who had set up his spider's network in a large cupboard from whose artificial light he seldom blinkingly emerged. Mostly he asked for his meals in his cupboard, and smiled shyly at her as she brought them in. He hardly ever spoke.

They made her enrol for the Open University for she refused to go to the local college for fear of being found and made to leave her adopted family. They heard her story and connived at her disappearance for they agreed she did right to scarper and anyway liked having her around, especially as she did all the shopping and enjoyed experimenting with their evening meals, which became a regular celebration in the house. They encouraged her to engage in further personal development for all believed firmly in PROGRESS. The one asleep always left his vote for house action on a note on the kitchen table as he went in or out. The nerd left word processed notes around. For some years she continued this happy existence. With their money and her flair she turned the squat into a palace and a place of elegant entertainment for their friends. She presided, cool and elegant, as hostess to all their functions. She was especially useful to the bandleader as he picked his way to success through agents and producers.

One day, when shopping in a street market for vegetables, she stopped to look at the bric-à-brac stall where she sometimes bought a bright thing for the communal home. She saw the woman next to her handling a blue plate and recognised the rings. Before she could swiftly go she had looked at the woman and found her mother's eyes in hers. She recovered herself first and ran but her mother caught her up by the traffic lights. She accepted her invitation to a coffee and neither referred to the last conversation they had had.

"Is my dad alright? Is Lochinvar OK?" said the daughter as they rose to leave and part. "Yes," said the mother, who had spoken to neither since the leaving. "Thank you. They are fine. And you? Have you a family now?" "Yes," said the daughter, "I could not wish for better." "That's nice," said the mother. And, after a long pause, "I hope you'll always be happy." I shall, said Blanche softly to herself as she turned away, as long as I don't go taking up with some bleeding prince. She never did. At her insistence, the squatters bought the house for cash for she became most particular about the regularity of her situations in life. She continued to preside over her idyllic set up and became as well a very famous barrister, specialising in family law until she finally took silk, and became a great judge. Even then she was home in time to prepare the evening meal for her family, the six awake and the one asleep.

Margaret Whyte.

XVIII

Cinders 3

"It is often safer to be in chains than to be free."

Kafka, *The Trial*, Chapter 8

An ambitious and successful businessman was suddenly left a widower. Although notorious as a tiger in the company, his role was different at home where he was dominated by his manipulative and attractive wife and totally devoted to their assertive only child, a daughter called Dominique, now aged 16. He was blessed with a skilful and understanding secretary, who provided him with the antidote to home by accommodating his non-professional needs in the exciting atmosphere of an illicit affair. Nevertheless, he took his wife's death badly, for he was not used to reflection. He was a doer, and unable to make sense of his reactions in this strange new world where his background assumed a new dimension, making unexpected calls for primary attention. His life became strange to him and all he wanted was to have it back the same as before.

To his surprise, his daughter, after the initial shock, seemed even more assertive and independent, no longer responding to offers to accompany him on the trips which were his way of paying attention and making amends for his long business days. On his return from the company, she was usually on the phone or, if it was later, either she would be out, or the house would be noisy with young strangers. He felt stranger and stranger and more and more depressed. He stayed out later and later at the office. His secretary, observing all this, stayed too. Her teenage girls had their own social life, and, since her divorce, she had long cherished hopes of one day becoming more than the accommodating secretary.

The widower was a pushover. After six months, marriage was proposed and accepted. The large house on the M4 corridor was easily big enough for another three persons and the widower expected no problem. He was vastly surprised by his daughter's reaction which all but lifted off the very substantial roof.

He went ahead with a quiet ceremony in the registry office, to which his daughter refused to come, and brought his new family home. His step-

daughters, Annie and Ella, were near in age and close. Their numbers did not weigh heavily in their favour in comparison with the fact that they were on the territory of a very fierce enemy indeed. Fortunately their mother had rented out their previous home as an income to support them through college and to this they insisted on returning. She could no longer continue in the company as wife of the boss, so was now in the desirable but dangerous position of a dependant on a rich man.

Dominique now raised the financial stakes. Her demands on her father to pay for her high and independent lifestyle could not be denied and as a minor her debts had to be paid. She was not used to being gainsaid. Her spending commanded attention from her father. Rather than returning his household to the comfortable backdrop to his work as he had intended, it had become a battleground. Photographs of his first wife appeared in every room on walls, ledges, furniture, in drawers, cupboards, pinned up on doors. And the new secretary at work had different ways, adding to his general discomfort.

In this kind of war, the tiger was a mouse and the new wife a piece of cheese. Every time he sought comfort from his wife, she complained about the last outrage from her stepdaughter. Dominique took her new dress, bought at vast expense for an important reception for an important client, to Oxfam. No new present from her husband lasted the week. Whatever room she was in, Dominique would enter alone or with her friends and put on their music loud. She put the phone down on her stepsisters and took no messages. To restore communications, the stepmother had to visit her own daughters in their house. Returning to that of her husband was becoming harder and harder. To the complaints relayed by her father, Dominique returned sweet reason and a gently injured air, sowing the seeds of further self-doubts and uncertainties in this minefield he had sown.

When his wife suggested that all this was not working and why should they not return to the status quo ante, so he could get back the secretary that had suited him so well and she could retreat into the safety of her own nest, he agreed with relief. An affair on the side suited both of them much better. What do you think of their chances of achieving that with each other now?

Margaret Whyte

XIX

Cinderella

"The answer was here all the time.
I love you, and hope you love me ".

Rice and Lloyd Webber, *Evita*

---

nce there lived an unhappy person called Cinderella. Her widowed father had remarried and she could not get on with her stepmother and two stepsisters. Her stepmother was disturbed by the likeness of Cinderella to the lovely portrait of her mother, a constant reminder to the husband of his first wife. Insecurity and jealousy made her unkind in a hundred subtle ways and her daughters followed suit, without the father appearing to notice or intervene. Cinderella was resilient and she had a sense of humour but she was a dependant and at times she found life quite hard to bear. Being increasingly ostracised she took refuge in busyness. She would scrub the kitchen floor with a hard brush and imagine that it was her stepmother's face she was scrubbing. She would clean the toilets and fantasize that it was her stepsisters who were being flushed away.

The kitchen was her favourite room. The family employed a cook. She was a curious old lady, but she taught Cinderella to cook, and she was Cinderella's only human friend. Cinderella had lots of non-human friends though she could not abide Mungo the cat. Fortunately, he was obese and was much too slow to catch the woodmice near the shed, or the newts near the cucumber frame or the brown rat who streaked past the back door on occasion.

It was party time. Time for Prince Charming to pick a bride from the social elite of the town. The town crier announced three balls, admission by invitation. Cinderella's father was a wealthy banker so it was not surprising that three invitations were delivered by hand for Miss Jemima, Miss Susannah and Miss Cinderella. "Of course you may go, Cinderella," said her stepmother, "but what will you wear?" Cinderella was too proud to appeal to her father. She tried to convince herself that a new dress and dancing and a buffet and a firework display were quite undesirable things really. She hoped that the old

moo would choke on her own bile as she scrubbed the kitchen floor practically to destruction.

However, when Cinderella saw her stepsisters, in all their finery, roll away in their carriage, chatting and laughing, her disappointment got the better of her. She headed down to the kitchen for the cheerful company of Mrs Muffin, the cook. She cried into the cup of tea that was handed to her in silent sympathy, salting her buttered digestive in the process.

"I shouldn't complain Mrs Muffin," she said, "but if I had a guardian angel, I'd ask for a new family who would make me welcome. I am sure I have tried to please my stepmother. I'm fairly certain it isn't my fault she doesn't like me. This ball, you know. It isn't that I'm interested in marrying the Prince. It strikes me as being a bit of a cattle-market. But I could have met someone nice. Mrs Muffin, why, Mrs Muffin, whatever are you doing? Are you feeling all right, Mrs Muffin ?"

Because Mrs Muffin had turned a sort of incandescent pinky-violety blue colour. She was shimmering and glimmering and eight digestives whirled in a sedate circle around her head like an edible halo.

"I hear your request, my dear Cinderella," she said, as she floated to the top shelf of the Welsh dresser. She plucked a digestive from her halo and crunched it thoughtfully. "You are a good girl and you deserve a break. You shall go to the ball."

We know what happened next. A pumpkin, some mice, two newts and last but not least, the brown rat were magically conscripted into being a carriage, horses and attendant staff. One final flourish of the half-eaten digestive and Cinderella looked supremely elegant in lilac silk embroidered with silver daisies. Upon her feet was a pair of glass slippers lined with lilac satin.

Mrs Muffin warned her to be home by twelve to make sure of arriving back first and Cinderella was driven away. One can only wonder what she thought about as she was driven to the palace.

Cinderella had a good time. She ate, she drank, she danced, she looked at pictures on the walls. She even danced with the prince three times but she did not find him particularly attractive. You might have thought the cachet of royalty would be enough. No, he had dull eyes. He had no spring in his step. She was honoured by the attention but found herself looking about. Shortly before midnight, her footman came to escort her to the waiting carriage. With a bow and a smile he handed her in. Looking into his bright and beady eyes she was struck by the realisation that this was her old friend, the rat. He was very nice looking in human form.

"Please sit and talk to me," she said, "I am not really a princess, so the informality doesn't matter if no one sees. Besides, we know each other."

"Indeed we do," he answered with another bow. "I have enjoyed many slices of gruyere and several pickled onions at your house, though I have not yet managed to reach the pâté. Luckily for me your cat is slow. I am somewhat disconcerted to find myself in human guise and it does feel quite heavy. However, I can now see that you are very pretty, and I'm sure you would make a delightful rat. In ratdom, I am called Wayne-Scott Ratmaninov."

"That is a very imposing nomenclature," said Cinderella, impressed.

"Well, we rats don't go a bundle on titles as you do. We rats stick together through thick and thin. I suppose you could describe us as a liberal republic. I am proud however, to be a member of the Ratmaninov clan. We have a distinguished history of service to our fellow rats. It was a Ratmaninov who saved several families in the Great Drain floods. In fact, our current Leading Citizen is a Ratmaninov," he added, diffidently. "That's my uncle Ratfink. I have lots of relations. We're very close."

By now, the carriage was nearly home. Mrs Muffin was waiting at the kitchen door. "Now tell me all about it dear," she said "But first I must tidy up." She made airy gesticulations with a tin of cocoa powder and Wayne-Scott Ratmaninov, the mice, newts and pumpkin resumed their natural identities.

(I am sure you know what is coming.)

Two sweaty balls later, the Prince was becoming seriously interested in Cinderella. Her step-sisters were all right, but nothing much compared to her. His eyes were now showing a mild spark, but the beady eyes of Mr Ratmaninov positively gleamed. And his tail swished most vigorously (when in rat-form).

"If you were a rat, my Cinderella," he said as they rolled homewards on the final evening, "how my mother would admire your energy and industry, my father appreciate your charm and all your pleasant ways, my sisters relish another amusing companion in our busy nest. We would gather feasts by moonlight. We would raise squeaking nestfuls of happy rat babies and wreak havoc upon our enemies."

"It sounds oddly good to me," replied Cinderella, "I will have to see what Mrs Muffin says."

Mrs Muffin raised no objection for this proposal was an answer, if an unlikely one, to Cinderella's prayers.

Cinderella lived very happily as rat citizeness. Her family were puzzled by her disappearance but they soon had greater worries. First Mrs Muffin resigned. Then they began noticing holes in their best cushions, clawmarks in their damask curtains, footprints in their pâté. And Mungo was useless.

K-E Hazeldine

XX

Babes 2

"It's an ill wind that blows nobody any good."

Traditional.

---

here was once a poor forestry worker whose wife died leaving him with two little children to bring up. As there was no chance of meeting women where he lived, he advertised in the personal columns of the local paper for a woman who liked the countryside and would not object to a ready made family of a boy and a girl, with a view to marriage. There were several replies and the forestry worker studied the letters wondering how to deal with them. Eventually he picked out two. One was from a girl of eighteen

...The alsation was preferable...

who asked if she could bring her Alsatian, and the other was from a divorcee who already had two children. The forestry worker asked his children to choose which they would rather have and without hesitation they said they preferred the dog. The girl was picked up on the following Sunday in his Subaru and the dog went in the back with the children. The girl said how she loved the country and wanted nothing better. She fished in her pocket and produced a tape which she looked to put in but there was no place so she fished again and this time out came a mobile phone. She proceeded with a lively and meaningless exchange with someone called Dave. Meanwhile, the forester studied her thigh length boots, fake fur jacket and numerous silver rings. He had not yet dared to look into her face for he had seen that it was both bold and pretty.

To his surprise, she seemed to settle in and was casually kind with the children whom she kept well supplied with bubble gum and discs for the music machine that was installed on the third day after her arrival. The dog was no bother but the kids preferred their father's casseroles to her offerings of supermarket stuffed pancakes and pot noodles.

One day the girl told them not to come straight home after school but to go and find their father and come home with him, but as they set off to that part of the forest where they assumed him to be, a muggy mist was rising from the ground and soon they could not even see the path. For all their familiarity with the forest trails they got lost and were wandering in wider and wider circles until they came to a clearing they did not recognise. There was a small deserted forester's house they seemed to remember from somewhere, but now there was a huge row of white plastic sheeting over some very tall spiky green plants that looked more like thickets they were so dense. The Subaru and the dog were outside the house. The kids assumed their father and girl were there but had no good feelings about knocking. They sat down in the mist to wait for them to come out and take them home. They waited a long time before the girl came out and got into the van. She started the engine and the children rushed over. She looked very fed up to see them and before she could speak two men came out of the house. Neither was their father. They grabbed the kids and she got out of the car. No one spoke to the kids but there were a few cold words the kids made no sense of and they were put into a small room with a boarded up window and told to stay there and they would be brought some fish and chips if they were good.

The girl and the men left, presumably to fetch the food, for the children heard the sound of the van drive off. But no one came back and the children were locked in the house. Nowhere could they get out. All the windows were not only boarded up but barred from the inside. There was no toilet, and only two old chairs and one long trestle table. They called and called and banged and shouted then wept. They could not imagine what had happened. They were very cold, and had to use a corner as a toilet. Then they noticed a box of matches on the broken mantel shelf and some loose floor boards. They used their exercise books for kindling and set fire to the floorboards in the fireplace. They had no idea if it was night or day and so they stayed till they were found three days later as they were told. The girl was not with their father and the police who found them. The police were very interested in the plants under the polythene and asked the children lots of questions about the men they had seen with the girl.

The children and their father resumed their lives without the girl. Some years later the forester's children went in search of the house in the clearing and found it. Kicking around in the dusty sunlight coming in the open door, they came across the missing floorboards and the charred bits still in the fireplace. Rooting around where the hole in the floor joined the skirting boards, they pulled out a rotten sackfull of dirty old bits of paper which they were going to burn until they saw what they were. Fivers and tenners and twenty-pound notes, hundreds of them. They lasted them nicely through college where they both did well and said nothing about the deposits making interest in their names, not even to their father, for who was to know what his relationship with the girl had been ? He never said. And now they knew what those plants had been.

Margaret Whyte

XXI

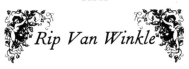 Rip Van Winkle

---

"The brain has many corridors . . . greater than material presence."

Emily Dickinson

---

 racy Higginbottom was a pretty girl from an ordinary working-class background, not particularly bright but pleasant and cheerful. She had little academic success at school but had secured a job as a checkout girl at Tesco. It was through this job that she met Hubert Van Winkler (pronounced Vinkeler). Hubert came from a banking family of Dutch descent although they now lived in Surrey. As a student Hubert lived in a cheerless bedsit in Camden and was immediately attracted by the bright and bubbly Tracy who had the added attraction of being a reasonably good cook.

When marriage was proposed, Hubert's family nearly had a fit. Of course they were not snobby, indeed Hubert's father had once nearly voted Labour, but Tracy, they agreed, really would not fit in – her accent was wrong, her education lacking, her dress sense cheap. It would, they insisted, be quite cruel to take that particular fish out of its water. They should have known that the more they objected, the more determined Hubert would become.

The marriage, surprisingly, lasted eight years. Tracy had made an enormous effort to learn the necessary etiquette, had an almost perfect accent and a wardrobe full of good clothes when Hubert's eye was caught by the daughter of a family friend. Tracy was doubly hurt by the fact that she had done her duty and very painfully produced a son now aged five.

After the divorce, Tracy and Edward, her son, were dispatched from the mansion in Surrey to a modest house in suburbia. To keep some semblance of pride after this mortification, Tracy forgot her humble beginnings and assumed airs and graces that cut her off from the local community. She adamantly refused to let Edward play out with the local kids – it was bad enough that he had to go to school with them.

At first, Hubert visited once a fortnight bringing presents for Edward. He eased his guilt by making these ever bigger and more expensive; Edward's favourites were his TV and video, his Sony Playstation and his up-to-the-minute

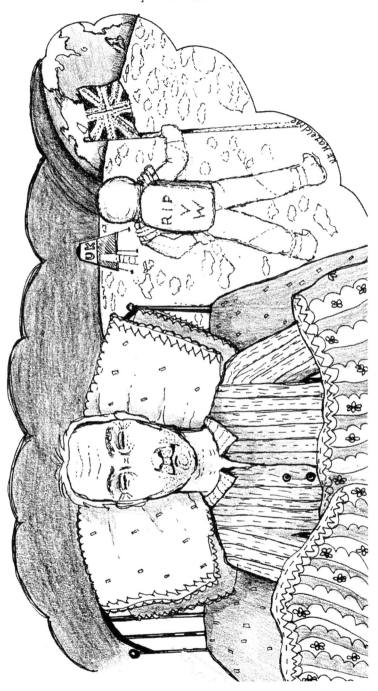

PC with the latest processor and peripherals. Hubert kept him supplied with videos, CDs and software, although as time passed these were usually sent through the post.

Watching videos or playing computers late into the night made Edward very sleepy during the day and when he was thirteen one of his teachers said "Edward Van Winkler. Rip Van Winkle. One of these days you'll wake up and find all of your life has passed." His classmates thought this was a huge joke and thereafter called him Rip. Edward didn't mind as Rip suited him well. It was a hero's name on a par with Troy, Buck and Clint, so Edward was more than happy for Rip to become his alter ego.

Next day, Edward sat in his maths class. The teacher was introducing the concept of graphs. Edward listened intently for a while until he gave the instruction " plot the equation x = y². " Rip instead heard Captain Kirk saying "Rip, plot course Alpha Zero Two Zero Two.", " Right away, Sir," Rip replied and away they warped through the universe. By the time the bell went for lunchtime, Rip had "boldly gone" into a previously unknown planetary system, prevented two races of aliens from embarking on an annihilatory war without any bloodshed whatsoever, (or whatever circulated in the aliens' bodies), and had totally convinced them of the advantage of democracy (or what passed for democracy in the late twentieth century in the USA.) In the meantime, Edward's graph paper remained a complete blank.

During the lunchbreak Edward sat by himself eating his sandwiches. Out of the corner of his eye he noticed two big boys pushing around a small boy. Rip immediately jumped up and placed himself between the bullies and their victim. Everyone in the playground gathered round and the tension could have been cut with a knife. "Huh," sneered the bigger of the bullies, "what have we here, a hero? Get lost loser before we do YOU some damage!" " Go ahead punk. Make my day!" growled Rip. Edward was completely unaware that, in reality, the small boy had reluctantly handed over his dinner money and was now in tears.

On the way home Rip passes two beautiful long-legged, long-haired girls. "Hi babes," he drawled. "Oh Rip," they swooned and stroked his arms. All the way home every male between the ages of thirteen and seventy eyed enviously the handsome hero, lucky enough to have a beautiful girl on each arm.

And thus Rip's life continued – an endless fantasy based on the videos, TV and computer games he so loved. He failed all his exams miserably but luckily for him his father, stepmother and their children were tragically killed in a plane crash and he inherited the mansion in Surrey and nigh on a million pounds. When his grandparents passed away he inherited more millions so he was never short of money. Edward as such ceased to exist and only Rip remained.

One person observed Rip's life. Rebecca had lived next to him in suburbia. She was the same age and in his class at school. Being of a sweet and caring nature, she felt drawn to the strange, quiet, friendless boy next door. She tried engaging him in conversation but he replied only in monosyllables and his attention was always elsewhere. Nevertheless, their lives ran along parallel lines and after a short, disastrous and childless marriage, Rebecca ended up keeping house for Edward in the Surrey mansion. Twice a week, she had coffee or drinks with friends in the village, where she would comment on poor Mr Edward. The paucity of his life, despite his wealth, appalled her. Her friends thought her very brave to dare to be in the same house with someone so strange.

When Edward died, Rebecca wept bitterly by his grave despite the fact that he had left his fortune to her. She and the vicar were the only mourners and tender-hearted Rebecca wept for what she thought of as Edward's pointless empty life and the loneliness and unhappiness she thought he must have suffered.

If only she'd known the truth! Edward had grown old but Rip stayed for ever young. As Edward had lain dying at the age of seventy-eight he was content. Rip thanked God for the wonderful life he had been privileged to live. He reflected on the breadth and depth of what he had seen and done. He had explored the galaxy, he'd experienced the range of human (and alien) emotions, he'd been loved, admired and adored by millions. He had fought the bad guys and won. He was, in short, a hero.

As Rebecca said her farewells to the vicar, she looked at her watch, and realised, thankfully, that she would be home in time for *Neighbours*. Lou and Cheryl were fighting over the custody of little Louise. She just had to know the outcome. Later, of course, there'd be *Coronation Street*. Kevin was having an affair. What would happen when Sally found out . . .?

Linda Thatcher

Such a quiet little man ......

XXII

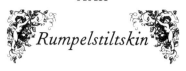

Rumpelstiltskin

"Deliver us from evil".

The Lord's Prayer.

omewhere not too far from here is a very quiet little man. His neighbours feel uncomfortable when they see him but as he never speaks he is easily avoided. They could not give a logical explanation for their reactions to him. No one can recall his arrival in the neighbourhood nor any family connection. His age is anywhere between thirty-five and fifty-five. He is taken for granted unless a specific question about his origins is raised, in which case a blank is drawn. It is obvious that he has no regular work from the times he is seen shopping in the local supermarket and sitting on the benches outside the local primary school. He takes no apparent notice of the mothers and children. No one ever asks for him, or calls at his house. He has a cat, which is huge and black and has a considerably higher profile in the neighbourhood than he does.

No one ever notices his absences of a day or two. One day as he sits on a bench outside the shopping square, another person sits on the same seat. She is a young girl in school uniform who folds her arms tight across her stomach and rocks, staring into space. After a while, she snatches up her bag and walks off. He follows her with his eyes and an expression of complete comprehension. The same time the next day, school lunch time, he waits on the same bench and she comes again. He notices that she eats nothing as she rocks for a while, catches up her bag and departs. As he has the gift of invisibility, she does not notice him, so she is not alarmed when he sits down at the opposite end of the bench when she occupies it a few days later. She still eats nothing as she sits out the lunch time.

The girl is oblivious to the fact that he has followed her home, has looked up the name of the occupants in the electoral register, has got the phone number. He watches the house, which is in a private road and has bay windows up and down overlooking a small front garden. No one notices his small grey person walking with no special step along the road and no one sees him look directly at the house.

A month or two later, as she begins to eat on the bench, and his searching eye has caught the change in her shape which even her own mother would not have seen, he sits quietly on another bench between two trees on the same side of the road as her house until one evening he sees a man and a woman in their late thirties come out and drive off in the Ford Sierra usually parked in their drive. He moves to the nearest phone box and when a girl's voice answers the phone, says he is a social worker who has heard that a baby is expected by an under-age girl and could he have a word with Mrs Sandford. There is a terrible long silence followed by distressed breathing and the receiver is replaced. The next time he sees her parents leave, he rings again asking to speak to Mr Sandford. The receiver goes down quickly. The next time he rings, it is mid-morning and he asks to speak to Miss Sandford. The mother assumes the call is for her as her daughter, Miss Sandford, was, of course, at school. The caller corrects her, leaves no message, and hangs up.

The mother questions her daughter on her return from school, as to the phone call. The little man watches the girl closely on the bench the following day and sees the panic in her rocking and now, at last, tears. "It is almost time," he thinks.

The next day he rings her mother again, asks for Miss Sandford as though he has not been told she is at school and again refuses to give his name or leave a message.

He watches the girl for the next two days until he sees she will not stay on the bench for another lunch time and follows her as she wanders blankly through the shopping centre. He watches from a shop doorway as she is greeted by and barely responds to two girls in the same uniform of about her own age.

As she sits on a seat in the crowded mall he sits next to her and says quietly, in his soft voice, "I can help you." She is so shocked, she stares at him. What does she see? A small grey man with deep eyes who is looking at her as though he knows her. "I know your problem. I have been trying to reach you," he repeats gently as she continues to stare.

"Do your parents know?" "No," she says. "They would kill me." The little man reflects on the use of cliché and never ceases to marvel at the sameness of human response. She is thinking, how stupid of me to admit it like that. I do not know him. He could be anyone. "There is no need for your parents ever to know. There is no need for anyone to know. This is a common problem which we are well used to sorting," he says.

"I don't believe in abortion," whispers the girl, "and I don't know what else there is."

"Of course you don't," agrees the small man. "How could you? You are only a little girl yourself. I expect you are about five months pregnant. Are you sure your parents do not know?" "No," says the girl. "They would never believe this could happen to me". "We must be sure that your parents do not know or suspect and could not hear from anyone else," persists the little man, "or we could not help." By now sobbing softly, the girl assures him that no one knows, she has told no one and she wishes she were dead.

"Dear me! you must not wish that," says the little grey man, in his soft voice. "Your problem is no problem at all. We deal with things like this all the time. Much much harder things than this." To the girl, nothing could be harder. She suddenly sees that maybe she could have a life after all. "You leave it all to me," says the little man. "Come here tomorrow at the same time and I will tell you what I want you to do." She is waiting for him. "Set out to school at the usual time tomorrow. We will ring the school and say you are not well. They will assume it is your mother. Come to the car park where you will be met by a man and a woman in a black BMW. If we help your baby to be born now, with assistance it will live. It will need a lot of special attention and afterwards it will be very well looked after by people who cannot have their very own baby. If the baby is born with help now, no one need know that you ever had one. We will bring you back to the car park by the time you would be coming home from school. What do you say to that?" The girl agrees immediately to everything and asks no further questions. All she knows is that she is going to be free with no penalties attached as far as she can see and she is not looking very hard.

The soft-spoken man is as good as his word. Next morning, she is at the car park. A man and a woman meet her. They go for a drive and stop outside a very big house. They all go in. The girl is led into a nice white room where a kind lady pricks her hand and she remembers nothing further. When she comes round the kind lady says everything has been taken care of and they will now take her home after she has had a cup of tea and a nice cake. On no account is she to say what has happened to anyone at all or the lovely people looking after her baby will not be allowed to keep it and it will be brought home to her house.

The girl fervently promises secrecy and is returned to the shopping mall car park where the clock shows 4 pm. Hometime from school.

She often, and as she gets older, increasingly often, thinks about her baby growing up happily with lovely people. She weeps often. Not as much as she would weep if she knew the true identity of the little man, the Great Sorcerer himself. And what HAS he done with the baby?

He is quietly getting on with his business. He is so helpful.

Margaret Whyte

XXIII

Bluebeard

> *"Lay your sleeping head, my love*
> *Human on my faithless arm."*
>
> W H Auden, *Lullaby*

 am leaving this letter to you, Anne, along with my will and other papers, which will be deposited in my bank which I have named as my executor. My husband is unaware of these arrangements for I tell him I refuse to think of such things and, in the event of anything happening to me, I am sure he would cope!

As you know, I always wondered why he chose me. I do not lack confidence in my attractions and abilities but I have to acknowledge that I am not in the same league as him in either of those departments. Despite your fears and the doubts of others, expressed with more or less finesse, I can say he has been an excellent husband and father. He is home as often and early as possible for a man in his position. He always gives me a good account when he returns from his business abroad and makes straight for the children with the ingenious and delightful gifts he brings after every absence, to console us for it, as he says like a litany. His ways are pleasant, witty, charming, especially with us.

I can hardly bring myself to the next bit. How could I doubt so lovely, so controlled and so affectionate a husband who makes me and the children the centre of his life amidst the demands on an international financier? He always seemed to work to live and for my part, throughout our brief courtship and the ten years of our marriage, I have never felt that I was importunate nor the children, as they came, anything but a total fascination for him.

It serves me right. Two years ago now, while he was sorting out the Hong Kong business, missing him, I took to going through the bureau in his study next to my reading room. Rummaging in the back, I caught my ring on something and a whole compartment appeared under the writing surface. There was a Victorian scrapbook with arched windows for the pictures, garlanded with wreaths of flowers. I did not recognise the young men in the photos which looked recent. They were all dressed the same in white T shirts,

your cup of tea derling

white shorts, white socks and boots. I would have said they looked like members of a rugby team but as I turned the pages and counted there were only eight. As you know, my husband is keen on rugby and it is now a family treat to go to Twickenham as often as we can since we took the box.

I did not recognise any of these young men, six of whom were black and two Asian. For the reason that he had never shown me this nor mentioned any people he had met who would fit the photos, I wished to return the album to its compartment under the shelf and had the very devil of a job trying to figure out how to replace it. Thanks to my knowledge of antiques, I finally managed the switch as in the attached drawing.

On that occasion, he was called unexpectedly to Jakarta, so I had a couple of days to think about the album. I concluded that there were so many possible explanations it was not worth thinking about.

When he returned we all went off to Geneva so he could combine business with us and it was some weeks after our return before his next trip, which was to South Africa. In his absence I returned to his album, but this time there was a new face, for I was positive I had counted only eight and now there were nine. The new one was Asian. The "uniform" was the same. So was the stance, with the arms crossed and the feet apart. They were all about seventeen, not younger, maybe a bit older. They were all very good-looking (have I said this already?). They look at the camera as though they know the photographer, despite their conventional pose. As they are individual they cannot be a team? After his return from South Africa, I wait till he is away again in KL and return to the album. A new face has appeared. It is of a splendid young black man, in the same rigout and pose. Now there are ten.

I do not know whether the nightmares that are starting are worse when he is with me or away. I cannot bring myself to speak to him about it. There was indeed an eleventh after the big meeting to sort out the arrangements in Seoul. That was when I could not get it out of my head and I do not know whether it makes it better or worse to get it down like this. Your cool head would be a great comfort to me now, or would it? I would be ashamed to share these fears face to face for they do not have a name or a shape. Will the first album take more? Will there be a second started ? Will that be the lot and some mysterious team complete?

How foolish I have been to give myself worries like this. The whole house shakes with fun at bath time. I look at his beautiful head with its glossy blue black hair next to mine. Some great artist should draw his long, lean, smooth and powerful body. A dark Botticelli. He smiles in his sleep and reaches out to draw me in. Like a great big beautiful cat. What have I done.

Postscript

My Aunt Anne left me this letter and other papers, as she wrote in her sensible and succinct way, "two albums later". I do not have the originals, as they were taken away by Interpol who came after my parents were killed in their Porsche which, so the coroner said, was driven at a speed of over a hundred miles an hour into a line of beeches in the New Forest, with my mother at the wheel. My brother and I were brought up by my aunt who did her best to shield us from the media and prepare us for our heritage as millionaires and orphans of some unimaginable and unspoken horror. She thought we should know at least as much about our own business as the public and that our mother was no suicidal drunken maniac who killed our father. Our memories of him are incompatible with that which never came to court.

Margaret Whyte

XXIV

The Frog Prince

For Beauty being the best of all we know
Sums up the unsearchable and secret ways
Of nature.

R S Bridges, *The Growth of Love*

---

fter the early death of her mother, the dark daughter of a powerful American merchant prince grew up in the care of her bodyguard and governess. These protected her from the harmful things of the world. On the positive side, her life was made even richer by an affinity with her father's library and the creations of the great artists with which she was surrounded. As a child, she ran in corridors lined with ancient marble replicas of her own kind, never since surpassed. She observed the soul of wild and powerful creatures as they writhed and lunged in their bronze prisons. Small perfect things lay on ledges, tables, shelves, in domes, cases, wherever her body or eyes could come to rest. Marvellous shapes of the things of sky and sea swung in the air of the high ceilings folding in and nurturing the light from thousands of electric candles. The daughter of the merchant prince knew from her cradle that the underpinnings of her world lay in subterranean machinations whose purpose was the ultimate worship of beauty. All else was the means to that end.

Her guardians were chosen for their loyalty, strength of mind, and high educational status, supporting some unexpected and hidden skills of a less cerebral kind. Their task was made more pleasant by the nature of the preoccupations of their charge who demanded their wholesale and vigorous companionship in her pursuit of beauty and the understanding to appreciate it. Her own rooms were hung with Raphaels, Botticellis, a Mantegna, two Gainsboroughs, and several Burne-Jones. Her intimate and personal companions were King Cophetua and the Beggar Maid, as they sat together but apart thinking their own thoughts, in the painting opposite her bed. They were the first people to be greeted at dawn and the last before she closed her eyes to meet them in her dreams.

Her father brought the greatest ornaments of the human race in terms of

mind and achievement to instruct her with their visions of the outward and inner appearance and essence of things, and they were pleased to accept the charge to spend some hugely paid time instructing this avid daughter of a magnate in his fantastic castle. She was thus educated in the most recent discoveries and insights into the Arts and Sciences with which to balance the power of the past reigning in the artefacts of the greatest genii of their times. At an age when other girls are beginning to be aware of their personal appearance and social image, she reflected on those of the whole space-time continuum of the civilisation which had produced her.

Accompanied by her guardians on her private jet, she made a playground of the great galleries of Europe. In Florence, one sweet day in early summer, she sat down in the gardens of the Medici-Riccardi palace to muse at a fountain. She watched the clouds break and reassemble in the water of the pool as she stirred it with her hand. Behind her she saw reflected a thin dark man, who seemed to move with difficulty as he threw a lily into the water before her. As she turned, he was gone. Her guardians, sitting nearby, had seen nothing and nobody. Yet the lily remained, beating on the edge of the retaining wall, caught in the rhythm of the fountain.

"Where have I seen that face before?" she wondered as they walked back through the cypress groves to the apartment purchased as part of some deal with an Italian prince. Sitting in its courtyard with her guardians for a twilit dinner of seafood and crisp pink wine, she thought she caught a glimpse of the face in the fountain. The lean dark features rimmed with a blue black shadow, the intensity of the dark eyes echoed her awareness of the great prince of the past whose territory she now occupies. She is reminded of the pull of his inward downward gaze and the lovely smile that no murderous pope nor appalling torturer commanding a rival kingdom can turn into the rictus of disappointment in humanity. She has long concluded that both he and her father were saved from the consequences of terrifying sin, by their appreciation of beauty in the eyes of other beholders. And were not both immortal by reason of their patronage of those whose work defined the achievements of their civilisation, even if financed from another, lower world?

As she looked over the silhouette of Brunelleschi's great dome in the green and violet sky, she pondered the relationship between wealth that made the Arts possible and the irony that the creation of the Sistine Chapel itself brought about the activities of the iconoclasts a century or so later. How could Savonarola have gained an ear in the Florence of Botticelli, still less that of that worshipper of worldly beauty?

In the darkening square below she sees the outline of a thin man sitting on a bench with one shoulder hunched. Regretfully she turns away from the remaining glory of the day to prepare in her dreams for the next. With all her appreciation of the works of the artists, she knows that to beg for the greatest gifts of the Gods for herself is to invite the disasters meted out to those of infernal impudence. Hers only to pay, not to do. A rich beggar among the Talents. As her father's only heir she knows it will be her duty to manage the products of Mammon for the benefit of those labouring for the Muses. She will profit from Machiavelli's advice to the Prince to keep the fingers of the courtiers in her father's palace off the Dragon's Hoard so that she may be present at the birth of the creations inspired by the Gods in the minds of the infinitely richer.

That night in her dreams Lorenzo holds out a lily, looking closely into her face. She looks back at the deep lines round his tensely smiling mouth. Deep within the petals of the lily, she sees the face of Raphael looking out. She knows then that a new Florence will rise in Oregon and she will bring it forth.

Next day her guardians are shocked to see how her face has suddenly darkened. That day, too, she begins to complain of pain in her joints. "We must get home," she says. "There is much to be done." The fax winging its way through the skies passes the homeward path of her jet.

In the great pink and white palace of the now dead merchant prince, her father, she wanders through the rooms, taking stock. She is not alone. "Never leave me," she whispers. "I have been waiting a long time," he says. "I have watched for you for centuries. Would you object to my presence in you? I was often told I am very ugly. It was my brother who was beautiful. I have tried to store myself in beautiful places as I waited."

"I can guess your last," she replied. Opposite her bed, the Beggar Maid sits alone.

Margaret Whyte

XXV

The Emperor's New Clothes

But the Devil whoops, as he whooped of old

It's clever, but is it art? Kipling, The Conundrum of the Workshops.

nce there was a great art gallery. It was built of modern materials according to the classical principle of the Golden Mean and it housed the most admired modern icons of Europe and the New World. Tens of thousands came every year to contemplate the Pollocks, the Rothkos, Klees and Rileys and all the other members of this illustrious firmament.

The Gallery was more than a vault for past creativity. The curator, Wencelas Cheroot, was committed, quite rightly, to the new, the young, the on-going. He prided himself on being avant-garde. Art must be conceptual, minimalist. Representation, craftsmanship, . . . these were defunct characteristics of Great Art in contemporary times. His values were reflected unremittingly in the Gallery's acquisition policy, and no artwork ever won the Great Annual Art Prize that did not provoke a controversy.

His policy became more extreme as time went on, to the extent that he disdained anything created by brushwork. Wencelas Cheroot was passionately keen on Installations, one of the earliest to achieve fame/notoriety being a neat ensemble of bricks. He was increasingly interested in sound/video Installations, and in Actuations, which involved some form of physical performance by the artist.

Recent winners of the Great Annual Art Prize had included a video actuation of a man dressed as a runner bean pedalling a stationary penny farthing. It was called "Supernature: Subnature". The year after that it had been a giant black pot and a giant black kettle suspended from a frame. There was a tape-recorder concealed inside the pot, and it bellowed the word "BLACK" at thirty second intervals. It was entitled "Smelted Ostrich". Last year, it had been a crystallised chicken with a duck's head and a peacock's tail. This one was statically housed in a blue perspex pyramid with a similar smaller pyramid next to it containing a brightly wrapped giant Easter egg. It was entitled "Chicken? and Egg?"

"We are seeing a cultural renaissance," announced the Curator at a press

conference called in the build-up to this year's Great Annual Art Prize. "Our collection is a simmering oasis of evolving potential that refuses to be repressed by hidebound views of the entity that is defined as being the world."

In the pause that greeted this declaration, the drawl of one of the Gallery attendants was clear, his words eagerly sucked up by thirsty microphones.

"Aw, haddaway and shite, man. We can aaall see it's just a heap of crap." (He was from Tyneside.)

"Of course," went on the Curator, as he narrowed his gimlet eyes at the traitor, while his bald head became shiny with rage, "wherever there is progress, there is obstruction, the most subtle and instructive being mental. Many artworks cease to be such if viewed from an altered viewpoint and vice versa, particularly in the case of the culturally challenged whom I invite to overcome iconoclastic prejudice by meeting the winning artwork halfway."

"What a divvy!" said the rebel, to the other attendants later. "He's the iconoclast, ya knaa. People come because they canna believe how bad it is! This place is full of taxidermy and effing sloppydadas. It's not Art."

Ho hum. *Not that debate again please*, I hear you say. Fair enough, this is only a story. Be that as it may, one iconoclast promptly sacked another for gross misconduct.

The prize winner was to be announced the following day, with maximum publicity of course, and Mr Cheroot and others worked very late that evening to ensure that the Great Annual Art Prize exhibition would be ready.

The next morning, crowds had gathered outside the building. Inside were journalists, a TV crew and the Mayor and many famous artists and critics. But, to the panic and misery of the Assistant Curator, there was no Wencelas Cheroot.

"Oh, God, how could you do this to me?" he whimpered, as he sent forth scouting parties and made desperate phone calls.

When the final countdown to filming began (the announcement was to go out live on TV) the unfortunate man accepted the inevitable. With a shaky flourish, he brandished the giant key that would unlock the Great Annual Art Prize gallery. He gave the signal and two attendants solemnly swung open the double doors. The cameras panned in.

The winning entry had been placed behind a screen and was mounted on a podium in the centre of the room. With ceremonial dignity, the attendants drew back the screen. People surged forward.

It was an Actuation. A figure was seated on a hobbyhorse. It was bound and gagged and on top of its head was a large, no, it couldn't be? . . . *something* of organic origin, something unsympathetic to the olfactory function, a thing not to be mentioned at dinner parties, yes, it was, it really was a turd! The figure struggled and writhed and its gimlet eyes reflected unspeakable anguish of body and spirit.

The piece was entitled:

"Creator:Curator: Apotheosis Of A Shitehead."

At first there was an astonished silence, and then . . . "Ingenious!" "A conceptual breakthrough!" "An admirable and courageous act of genesis!" cried the critics.

It took a while for the fascinated audience to realise, after much footage had rolled, and many flashes had gone off, that the figure was Wencelas Cheroot, and that he was not intentionally suffering for the sake of Art. He had been attacked late the previous evening by a masked man with marigold gloves, a giant roll of sellotape and a pail.

When he was finally released he created an almighty stink, and also, a furore.

Alas. His credibility was colonically and conclusively compromised, however many contemporary watercolour landscapes he authorised, and he bought a great many after this.

_____

K-E Hazeldine

XXVI

Nancy's Story

"Be not forgetful to entertain strangers:
for thereby some have entertained angels unawares."

Hebrews 13,ii

---

single mother, Nancy lived in a caravan with her kids. The family was not isolated for she was a New Age Traveller and lived with three other families in a wood. They were augmented from time to time by larger travelling groups who found a ready welcome and a good water supply in a quiet glade where the landowner was not hostile. Indeed, he often joined his guests round their campfire in the good weather.

Nancy worked hard as a software designer and desk-top publisher and recompensed her kind landlord for the site and the electricity by doing his accounts and drafting his difficult, time-consuming and often acrimonious correspondence with the Ministry of Agriculture and Fisheries. Such services he found more than acceptable payment. She was also a good artist and sold her miniature landscapes and wild animal vignettes at local fairs. She paid for the latest software educational packages for the children by doing astrological charts and reading the tarot cards. There were another seven children from the other families, whose parents also bucked the common expectation of the ignorant public by earning their living writing nature columns for establishment papers, devising origami packages, collecting and drying wild grasses, and providing a supply of amphibians for a research laboratory investigating the processes of cell regeneration.

The Education Authorities and the Social Services Department had long ceased to trouble the little community.

One March day, made hateful by squalls, a lone traveller came to the community. He was very tall and thin, with a face like a contented wolf, and was dressed in moleskins. There was something archaic about his appearance. He was very softly spoken as he asked permission to erect his tent in their midst. He explained that he was a molecatcher by trade but was on his way to a festival of folk music in the mountains of Wales. He produced his panpipes and played

his songs at he sat alone by his fire, until the children, beguiled by the haunting sounds, joined him.

That evening, Nancy had arranged to go to the House to return and discuss the correspondence with her landlord and as usual had asked the other parents to include her children in their care until she returned. The stranger had eaten. The children were listening to his music as the tempest had died down. Nancy would not be long. When she returned, the younger children were in bed and Jake, her eldest son, was surfing the internet for information on tree galls, which he intended writing up for a nature magazine. Her two elder daughters were presumably with their friends in one or other of the caravans. The stranger had retired to his tent where his silhouette showed by the light of his lamp.

After an hour, Nancy asked Jake to fetch his sisters. Sarah returned with him but Sue, the family angel, was not with her nor the other family. The five adults came together instantly and called out the stranger to search, for Sue had left no word and had not been seen by anyone since she had put the little ones to bed some time ago.

By midnight and no Sue, panic had set in. Nancy called in the landlord and summoned the police on her mobile phone. They were fast there with dogs and storm lanterns and powerful infra-red torches to search the woods. Details were collected from all the twenty people from the community, including the little children, while the search got under way. No Sue. At daybreak a desperate group sat round a communal fire which spluttered in the drizzle. The stranger was asked to accompany the police to the local station where he could be questioned about his movements. His belongings were left behind and a policewoman was seen to enter his tent and stay there a while.

Helicopters and the people from the local village joining in the intensifying search failed to add anything to the total blank drawn. Frogmen were diving in the deep ponds of the forest, screened off as discreetly as possible. The media were present with lights and cameras interviewing anyone available from the families. The adults were numb but the children were excited and had to be hauled away from the centres of their stage. Night fell on that day and the next, but no one slept. The police were inching the ground, by now some distance away. The dogs worked hard but gave no sign. The stranger returned from the police station, collected his things silently, expressed with great gentleness his confidence that all would turn out well, and cleared the camp.

After three weeks, an open file was kept for Sue, and the presence of the search faded from sight. Only the dreadful burden of ceaseless speculation buzzed in the heads of those concerned. The little ones stopped asking questions. Nancy sat dumb before her computer. Jake now took over his mother's outstanding tasks and surfed the net for missing persons. His mother was stirred by him to watch him set up a website with a MISSING SUE page kept permanently open. Months passed. One of the families, unable to bear the strain further, summoned a tow to a camp in the North and said tearstained and embarrassed farewells.

One day, long after it was looked for, there was an E- mail. Some two years ago a family, living an alternative lifestyle like them, had lost a son aged fifteen. Some time after, he had returned with no explanation. Since then, he had returned briefly then disappeared again. The link between the two cases was the sudden appearance of an unknown man whose description tallied with the molecatcher.

The police were called in to follow up this connection but could get no further. The molecatcher had also disappeared. According to witnesses, he had arrived for the Welsh festival but none could remember his leaving nor had any heard of his further destination. The search for him was intensified through the media, but even the popular programmes appealing to the public for feedback yielded nothing.

When dead hope itself had become a constant burden, deepening footsteps and lowering the voice, when life had settled into a new and joyless normality, when bills began to be paid again as Nancy settled sadly to her worldly commitments, when the sun shone on the dewdrops of a May morning, Sue came walking home. She was dressed as she had been when she disappeared. None could get her to say where she had been. She would only say, "I have been somewhere wonderful. I cannot tell you now but one day you will understand. We shall all reap the benefits." They all felt strangely comforted so that when she disappeared again some months later they were neither anxious nor distressed.

This time there was no return and as time went on the messages from other families on the internet who likewise suffered, built up into a growing folder of missing persons who had an alternative lifestyle in common. It was always the second child who went missing. All returned once. None ever said where they had been. All had contact with the molecatcher. All were specially loved by their family and friends for their sympathetic intuition, generosity and joyful disposition. Occasionally the media did a feature on the mystery which joined that of UFOs, kidnap by aliens, spontaneous combustion and other puzzling phenomena to be gathered into compendia for coffee table publications.

Jake became increasingly withdrawn, and, although he completed commissions for his mother as she required, he often had a faraway look in his eyes that disturbed her. One day Nancy accessed his records and found lists of contacts which she was unable to get onto the screen. One day, as he was out dealing with a client, she accessed his notebook and found an address not listed elsewhere. The screen filled with messages giving details of the children and her. Birthdays and details of presents , illnesses, deaths, contracts, the death of the landlord, births of children unknown to her, mysterious destinations with unexplained dates, tumbled out by the metre. The thing was, they were all in the future, some very far away.

When she spoke to Jake some time later, having had time to reflect, he silently moved to the screen and produced a title page. It said simply "MESSAGES FROM SUE". He indicated his younger brother and sisters. "These know before I do," he said. "They don't need this now," indicating the screen. "There are thousands of them out there now. The transmitters, I mean, like Sue, and those who receive them. You could call her a sort of guardian angel. They are recruited all the time. She is only practising as yet, with the future. What to do with it and us. That is why she is only dealing in the trivia of detail. She is learning how best to use her powers for us and the other commitments she has. It is a long apprenticeship and she dare not make mistakes. We are very lucky to have had her with us before in the usual way. We will be even luckier when she qualifies, or whatever they call it. As a career move, it was right for her, don't you think?"

Nancy reflected. After a while, she set out to surf under keyword "ANGEL". "Well, I would never have expected it to be a job like others with a recruiting officer, training schedules and so forth," she thought. "That's why we do not feel her loss. We have our very own guardian angel now." She asked Jake to ask why they had been given this privilege when they were aware of no great need, until the disappearance of Sue. The answer surprised her. "It is the family who is selected for their strength. The Angel is chosen because he or she can transmit it from them to others."

Nancy and her other kids continued with their lives in the wood, in contact with the worlds, on earth and in the heavens.

Margaret Whyte

Appendix

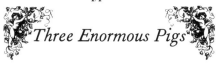

Three Enormous Pigs

nce upon a time, there lived a mother pig, who had three enormous children. Such was the greed of these pigs, her children, that one day their mother could cope no more and she said, "Look, my sons, you're nearly twenty. Most other pigs your age have a job by now, but you don't. You just sit around here stuffing yourselves. I want you out of the house by tomorrow." The three enormous pigs looked a bit downhearted but agreed to go.

The three pigs left the next morning, with a few coins each. As they left, their mother said, "Stay clear of the wolf. He's got a terrible cold."

The pigs, however, were not only very greedy, but impatient and impolite, and because of this, heard only the first half of the sentence, as they had trotted off before their mother could get the other half of the sentence out. In their twenty year existence the pigs had seldom left the house, as it would have interrupted one of their ten meals a day, and as a result the pigs had never seen a real wolf. The only thing they knew about a wolf was what they had read in a ridiculous fairy story, " The Three Little Pigs" in which the wolf is a violent type who eats little pigs. The wolf living in their area could not have been more different. He was a kind, gentle wolf. He was a vegetarian and the pigs' mother's secret lover.

Anyway, the pigs set off to look for a house. After an hour's searching the pigs came upon a pedlar. Realising that he would not be able to buy a house, the first pig said, " Pedlar, give me some straw." The pedlar, although taken aback by his rudeness, gave straw to the pig. The second enormous pig said, "Pedlar, I want some straw too." The pedlar replied, " I'm afraid I gave all the straw to your brother. I have some sticks though." "Those'll do," the pig said and he snatched the sticks from the pedlar. The third enormous pig said, "I want some sticks too." The pedlar replied, "I'm afraid I gave all my sticks to your brother. I have some bricks though and . . ." The third interrupted him, saying, "Give us them then." The pedlar left in a hurry never wishing to encounter such rudeness again and the three enormous pigs all left to build their houses.

The wolf came by that afternoon and walked up to the straw house of the

The young McPiggits yearn for new challenges and decide to leave home.

first pig, calling out, "Fat pig, please let me in." The pig in fright just put his head in his hands. The wolf then, with a sniff and a snort, sneezed and blew the house away. The pig just rolled as fast as his belly could carry him to his brother, the second pig, in his house of sticks. The wolf followed him, sneezing all the way.

When he arrived, he said, " Fat pigs, please let me in." They replied, "No," and just sat nervously in the house. The wolf then, with a sniff and a snort, sneezed and blew the house away. The two enormous pigs then rolled down the hill as fast as their two bellies could carry them to their third brother's house made of bricks. The wolf followed, once again sneezing all the way.

He arrived, and once again pleaded, " Fat pigs, please let me in." The fat pigs just looked out of the window and mocked the wolf, believing themselves to be safe. The wolf then, with a sniff and a snort, sneezed. The house, however, stayed upright. The wolf then knocked quite hard on the door. The enormous third pig in his laziness had not bothered with cement and as the wolf knocked on the door the house collapsed and the three enormous pigs were crushed.

The wolf returned to the house of Mrs Pig, received the aspirin for his headache he had been wanting from her sons all afternoon and married her and they both lived happily ever after.

Quentin Hughes